T. Gwynn Jones
The Great Deed of Gwilym Bevan

Thomas Gwynn Jones (1871-1949) is one of the major literary figures of the Welsh language. He is best known as a poet, in which capacity he won the Chair at the National Eisteddfod in 1902 and again in 1909. However he was also a prolific writer of prose, completing eleven original novels, including *Gorchest Gwilym Bevan* which first appeared as a serial in *Yr Herald Cymraeg* during 1899 and was published as a book later in the same year.
A new Welsh edition was published by Melin Bapur books in 2024.

This English translation is the first time *The Great Deed of Gwilym Bevan* has been made available in English, and the first publication in book form of an English translation of any novel by T. Gwynn Jones.

Translated from Cymraeg
This series aims to bring the literary classics of the Welsh language to new English-reading audiences for the first time.

Cover Design:
©Melin Bapur, 2024

Cover image:

Mihály Munkácsy (1844-1900)
Sztrájk (Strike) (1895)
Image in the public domain.

Copyright of the text in this volume:
©Melin Bapur, 2024

All Rights Reserved. No part of this book may be
reproduced or used in any manner without written
permission of the copyright owner,
except as a part of a book review.

ISBN:
978-1-917237-00-0

T. Gwynn Jones

The Great Deed of Gwilym Bevan

Being the novel *Gorchest Gwilym Bevan*
Translated from the Welsh by Adam Pearce

Melin Bapur: *Translated from Cymraeg*
General Editor: Adam Pearce

Thomas Gwynn Jones (1871-1949) in his early
thirties, during his novel-writing period.

Image reproduced with permission
from Gwynedd Archives.

Contents

Introduction

T. Gwynn Jones holds as good a claim as any to being the most important literary figure of his age writing in the Welsh language. Born in Mynydd Hiraethog in rural north-east Wales in 1871, he was the son of a tenant farmer who had been turned out by the landowner after voting against him in the 1868 British General Election (the first following a significant expansion of the franchise, but before the introduction of anonymous voting). As a child Gwynn, as he is usually referred to, was given such education as was normal for a boy of his class, including personal experience of the notorious 'Welsh Not', a punishment designed to encourage the learning of English by punishing children who spoke Welsh in school. Despite his teachers' best efforts he showed a great aptitude for learning however, and was ultimately offered a scholarship to study at Oxford University: a significant achievement for a boy of his background. Unfortunately, he proved unable to take up the offer following the first of a number of periods of prolonged ill health (both physical and mental) which were to plague him throughout his life. Whilst he could hardly be said to have been raised in poverty, these early injustices and failures help explain the man and the artist he would soon become.

Once he had sufficiently recovered, Gwynn found work in Caernarfon as a journalist for the flourishing Welsh press of the 1890s. This work, one way or another, was to occupy him for the next twenty years, and it was alongside his journalistic work (and in no small part to help fill newspaper columns) that Gwynn began to publish, first short stories and then, beginning in 1897, his first novel, *Gwedi Brad a Gofid* (After Treachery and Worry). But it was as a poet which Gwynn truly wished to be known, and his first volume of poetry *Gwlad y Gân* (The Land of Song, a popular epithet for Wales) appeared around the same time: a brilliant piece of satire, the poem of the title took aim at what he saw as the overly stuffy, formalistic and amateurish Welsh literary establishment, particularly the institution of the Eisteddfod. In the 1890s he also became involved with *Cymru Fydd*, the proto-nationalist movement within the Liberal party which campaigned for Welsh Home Rule.

As a writer, Gwynn was enormously prolific during his journalistic years. Between 1890 and 1910 he produced perhaps two to three hundred short stories, eleven wholly original novels, another five that were partial adaptations or translations, and many hundreds of poems; all alongside what must have been an unimaginable quantity of journalism, much of it published anonymously and now lost[*]. He finally achieved the literary recognition which he had always craved in 1902 when he won the Chair[†] at the National Eisteddfod; convinced he would not win, he was in fact absent from the ceremony, attending a wedding. The poem which won the competition, *Ymadawiad Arthur* (the Departure of Arthur) remains perhaps his best known individual work, masterfully blending elements of the native Welsh tradition with the European Romantic tradition that had grown up around King Arthur. But whilst the poem's

---

[*] It is only thanks to Gwynn's own meticulous cataloguing of his creative output that many of his stories and even some of his novels can be attributed to him.

[†] The Chair is the most prestigious of the awards at the National Eisteddfod and is won by the writer of the best *awdl*—an epic poem in strict *cynghanedd*, the complex poetic metre of internal rhymes and consonantal repetition unique to Welsh.

subject matter was medieval, its form was anything but. Not only was it considerably shorter and plainer in language than the typical Eisteddfod *Awdl* of the time, but Gwynn's use of the form to tell a narrative story was almost unprecedented, though it was a technique that would be followed by many others. Gwynn's victory was a significant early milestone in what was a new Romantic era in Welsh poetry, with Gwynn one of its central figures alongside W. J. Gruffydd, John Morris-Jones, R. Silyn Roberts, Hedd Wyn and others, which can now be seen as part of the swansong of Romanticism across Europe which took place in the years preceding the First World War[*]. Ironically, Gwynn cared little for *Ymadawiad Arthur*, though he did revise it several times later in his life, and his later epic narrative poems tend to avoid the *awdl*, instead developing new epic verse forms.

Gwynn continued to write extensively throughout the 1900s and in one year alone, 1907, appears to have published four novels and over one hundred short stories. This rate of work was not sustainable and another period of ill health led him to take a long trip to Egypt, where (characteristically) he turned his hand to yet another genre of writing and produced what is one of the earliest truly excellent pieces of travel writing in Welsh.

On returning to Wales Gwyn picked up where he left off; he continued to publish poetry, stories and novels and a second Eisteddfod Chair followed the first in 1909.

---

[*] In Wales the movement reached its apotheosis and its effective end and when the young poet Hedd Wyn won the Chair at the 1917 Eisteddfod with his lushly Romantic awdl *Yr Arwr*, (The Hero), having been killed on the battlefield a few weeks earlier. The Prime Minister Lloyd George was present at the ceremony and had just delivered a jingoistic speech from which Gwynn had stormed out in disgust. After the war, Gwynn and many of the others began writing poetry with a more modernistic inflection.

However, tired of the constant pressures of working in journalism, he sought a change of scene and found work as an archivist in the National Library of Wales in Aberystwyth. Whilst the change of pace was good for his health, a man of Gwynn's talents was wasted on such work, but his close proximity to the (still new) University gave him the opportunity to carry out research and lecturing work, and in 1919 he was finally appointed to a teaching position in the School of Welsh, and subsequently made a lecturer: a remarkable achievement for a man without an undergraduate degree. He was to remain there until his retirement, producing a great deal of important academic work, particularly on medieval Welsh literature. Whilst he had largely given up on writing creative prose after 1910 he continued to publish poetry, producing many of his finest poetic works in his last decades; he also translated extensively, translating Goethe's *Faust* into Welsh along with stories from Irish, which he spoke fluently alongside Breton, French, Italian, German and, of course, English and Welsh.

An attempt was made in 1926 to nominate him for a Nobel Prize for Literature, however he refused to allow himself to be nominated, believing himself, with customary self-doubt, to be unworthy. Had he accepted the nomination he would have been the first Welsh writer so honoured; in the event it was not until 1970 and Saunders Lewis that a writer in Welsh would receive a Nobel nomination.

Gwynn's status as a major poet and academic in the Welsh language is utterly assured. It is this version of Gwynn which is most familiar to Welsh readers: the medievalist, the strict-metre poet, the Romantic; the version we see in the anonymous portrait painted of him as an elderly university professor, perhaps left a little behind by his age.

Remarkably however, his prose, which is all the work of a young man in his twenties and thirties, has received very little recognition and is often glossed over or even ignored in most summaries of his work. Alan Llwyd describes him as the 'uncle' of the Welsh novel (Daniel Owen being the father), but it is difficult to claim that Gwynn was a particularly influential novelist as his novels appear to have been rather forgotten, even within his own lifetime. Even today, most of his novels remain unpublished since their original (often anonymous) serialisations.

It is initially difficult to explain why this might be. Certainly, Gwynn wished to be remembered first and foremost as a poet. He had stopped writing prose altogether once moving to Aberystwyth, and whilst two of his novels, *Lona* and *John Homer* did receive belated publications in the 1920s (almost twenty years after they had been written) he did not seem particularly eager to see this aspect of his legacy promoted. *Wedi Brad a Gofid* and *Gwilym Bevan* had been made into books in the 1890s but Gwynn's eleven other major prose can only be read in newspapers at the time of the present publication.

As with any similarly prolific artist, it is fair to acknowledge that there are lesser works in amongst the great ones. However, any suggestion that Gwynn wrote his novels and stories merely to fill newspaper columns will not long survive an examination of the works themselves. These are serious works, with Gwynn offering social and political commentary alongside often gripping stories. At their best, his novels are structurally tight and disciplined; his prose is readable and concise; his dialogue natural; his plots full of memorable set-pieces and exciting twists. Perhaps most appealingly of all to readers today is the way his own values of fairness, justice, integrity, tolerance and pacifism permeate his novels: Gwynn was an anti-imperialist in an age of jingoism, and a voice for religious tolerance and understanding in an age of bigotry. He wrote on subjects which Welsh writers had rarely before touched such as industrial action (in *Gwilym Bevan*), and even writing what is almost certainly the first science fiction novel in Welsh (*Enaid Lewis Meredydd*). In fact his novels are so immediately appealing today, and so lacking in many of the faults that plagued many of his contemporaries writing novels in Welsh, that their continued neglect begs an explanation.

To understand it, one must consider the wider context in which Gwynn wrote his novels. The novel was adopted relatively late in Wales, William Ellis' *Y Bardd* of 1830 usually considered the first example of the form in Welsh. Occasional examples followed over the next few decades (few of much literary interest) but it was not until the 1880s, and the success of Daniel Owen (1836-1895), widely acknowledged as the first significant novelist in Welsh, that the genre really took off. Novelists in Welsh had to battle against various prejudices: first the prominence given to poetry over prose in the Eisteddfod tradition; secondly, a puritan suspicion against recreational literature generally in a society much more religious than England at the time; but thirdly an obsession with the idea that a novel needed to justify itself by 'doing good' to its reader, either by teaching a useful lesson or otherwise modelling good moral values. Tied into this latter idea was an anxiety about the way these novels might portray Wales. One reviewer of William Llywelyn Williams' *Gŵr y Dolau*, published in the same year as *Gwilym Bevan*, wrote:

> We do not know of anything more distinctively Welsh in tone and character than this volume. In our opinion, it is more

> faithfully a reflect [sic] of Welsh life than even
> *Rhys Lewis...*

This kind of national anxiety is not uncommon for stateless, minority language cultures experiencing both a constant sense of being under threat and a constant need to justify themselves. "It must be characteristically Welsh before it will be of value to England and to the world," said O. M. Edwards of translating Welsh literature. In Wales' case more specifically, this anxiety was probably exacerbated by the way the Welsh were so often badly- and under-represented in English literature: Welsh characters, where they appeared at all, were often slapstick comedic characters speaking a broken English that did not reflect the way anyone in Wales actually spoke.[*] Stereotypes of the Welsh as being dishonest and worse were extremely common in the wider British press, and then of course there were the notorious Blue Books, the 1847 report into the state of Education in Welsh schools. This report had made many legitimate criticisms of poor educational practices, but also took aim at the supposed loose morals of Welsh women, and described the Welsh language as a backwards symptom of the nation's supposed lack of culture. The report was a cataclysmic event in Welsh history whose repercussions would reverberate for decades. An introduction like this one could not possibly begin to detail its impact, but with regards novel-writing it is sufficient to say that there were some who felt that novels could be one means to portray an alternative, more positive and wholesome vision of Welshness, particularly one informed by Christian morality.

---

[*] Shakespeare has a lot to answer for; this trope begins with 'Fluellen' in Henry V.

The most popular novel of the nineteenth century in Welsh, Daniel Owen's *Rhys Lewis*, perhaps exemplified this ideal, and then very probably reinforced it. The tale of a young man in poverty who becomes a minister, it ran into several editions and made its author a celebrity of whom a bronze statue now graces his hometown; but most readers today will prefer Owen's later novel *Enoc Huws*. A comedy about a con-man and a shopkeeper, it is a novel both more psychologically complex and more carefully constructed than its predecessor. Indeed, it is a superior novel by almost any measure, but lacked the didactic quality of *Rhys Lewis* to 'do the reader *lles* (good),' as contemporary reviewers often noted.[*]

Measured against this ideal it becomes easier to see why Gwynn's novels failed to capture the Welsh imagination. As a novel written in Welsh in 1899, *The Great Deed of Gwilym Bevan* (*Gorchest Gwilym Bevan*) was nothing short of a bolt from the blue. It opens with a suicide attempt (one of two in the novel) and also features a fire, a riot, a standoff with a pistol, a main character with religious doubts, a minister actively portrayed as a hypocrite, and various characters' deaths. No wonder the public didn't know what to make of it. At this stage Gwynn was twenty-eight, and if readers knew him at all it was as the young hell-raiser who had satirised the Eisteddfod tradition in *Gwlad y Gân*, or from his journalism. Clearly, here is an author who does not feel constrained to write only of those things which are respectable. Read any of Gwynn's novels from the perspective of what had come before him and several things are immediately apparent: that his models are not

---

[*] Various English translations of both novels are available; the best is the late Les Barker's translation *The Trials of Enoc Huws*.

Welsh[*], that his ambition far outstrips his contemporaries, and that what he wanted to give his audiences was very different from what they wanted to read. These are all things that both help explain his neglect, but also mark him out in retrospect as a major voice in the Welsh language novel.

Enough, then, about what this novel isn't, and time to say a little more about what it is. As has been noted, Gwynn had been inoculated against injustice from a young age, and viewed his poetry and prose as well as his journalism as a kind of activism. *The Great Deed of Gwilym Bevan* may be one of the earliest literary expressions of radical politics in Welsh. Here is a young writer determined to use his art as social and political activism, and not interested in pandering to anyone. Its deliberately vague setting (Treganol translated means 'Middle-town') could be any of the towns of the slate quarrying industry of North-West Wales, nestled between the mountains of Eryri and the sea. As well as being, as they still are today, the core of the Welsh speaking community, these industrial towns were hotbeds of political radicalism. It is tempting to think that the novel might have been inspired by the Great Strike at Penrhyn Quarry in Bethesda, an event of great significane which provided the backdrop for a number of later novels in Welsh[†], but the novel predates the strike by about a year. Local industrial disputes were fairly common but *Gwylim Bevan* is the first

---

[*] Titles like *Wedi Brad a Gofid* (After Treachery and Worry) and the wonderfully alliterative *Rhwng Rhaid a Rhyddid* (between Need and Freedom) are nothing like those of any earlier Welsh novels, and evoke Dostoyevsky and Austen, which gives you a clue. Gwynn would later abridge and re-write Tolstoy's *War and Peace* in Welsh (*Hedd a Galanas*).

[†] Most famously T. Rowland Hughes' *Chwalfa* and Kate Roberts' *Traed mewn Cyffion*, both available in English translation.

Welsh novel to really make a strike the centre of the narrative. In his excellent biography of Gwynn, Alan Llwyd describes *Gwilym Bevan* as a 'socialist' novel, and it certainly wears its political heart on its sleeve. Gwynn had turned to socialism after the failure of *Cymru Fydd*, and at one point considered standing for the Labour Party as a parliamentary candidate (though he was probably too uncharismatic and argumentative for politics). The novel is full of powerful expressions of radicalism that might almost be political slogans, such as Arthur's cry in Chapter X:

> I would rather die without a penny to my name
> than think that what I owned had been earned
> through ruining the lives of my fellow man!

However, it would be a mistake to assume that this novel is a black-and-white morality tale about the good workers and their evil masters. For a start, the tables are turned several times over the course of the novel: whilst he is indifferent to his workers' concerns, the Quarry owner Mr. Morrus is a character with various admirable qualities, and by the end of the novel appears to have fully realised the folly of his actions and indeed has suffered more than anyone else as a result of them. The workers, too, honest as they may be, are shown to be capable of brutality and savagery, and are quick to abandon their leader and make him the scapegoat for their grievances. In fact, rather than a theme of social solidarity, time and time again we see characters who are misunderstood by their peers and persecuted by them, whatever their class. Although undoubtedly radical, this is not a novel about class warfare, but about the struggle of the individual against society. Understanding this enables us to reconcile this novel with the absence of obviously socialist ideas elsewhere in Gwynn's creative output, and places *Gwilym Bevan* much closer to the Romantic mainstream of its author's work.

The novel does not end, as one might expect, from a 'socialist novel' with the workers victorious, nor crushed under the heel of the oppressor either. Instead, there is a final compromise, and a sort of collective social healing achieved by Gwilym's 'Great Deed', which is in fact a transfer of wealth *back* to the capitalist Mr. Morrus, that he might open the quarry once more (even if he will now pay the men more). This is the action which gives the story its title, a fact which should steer us away from a straightforward Marxist interpretation of the novel. At least one contemporary reviewer, writing in the *London Kelt*, found this ending deeply unsatisfying:

> I find it hard to believe that the story teaches
> the lesson intended, for it appears that it is the
> cruel owner who is rewarded in the end: after
> all the conflict it is he that gets all the wealth
> and a happy life

It is hard to see how a man who has lost both his children is to be understood to be living happily ever after; but regardless, the reviewer is missing the point: the lesson of compromise, reconciliation and forgiveness is exactly what Gwynn intends. Rather than undermining its message, this more nuanced lesson is part of what makes the novel far more than just a Marxist parable.

Besides his politics, a number of other elements from Gwynn's own life and background make their way into the novel, and although the narrative is mainly in the third person Gwynn's own voice can clearly be heard throughout the novel. We see his solidarity with suffering and his political radicalism most obviously; but more mundanely we see things like his contempt for poor journalistic standards (at the beginning of Chapter VI) and his ambivalence towards University education in characters such as Calfin Jones and Richard Morrus. Welsh cultural prejudice against novels comes under fire too, in Chapter V. Gwynn's own cosmopolitanism is front and centre, as are his love for learning (actual learning, as opposed to mere education), and his contempt for those who deem anything beyond their own knowledge and understanding, particularly anything foreign, to be dangerous.

Less obvious perhaps is how the novel reflects Gwynn's experience of depression. Throughout his life Gwynn was plagued by periods of anxiety, depression, pessimism and intense self-doubt, and whilst *Gwilym Bevan* cannot be considered a work of deep psychological complexity, the frank depictions of suicide and despair that it contains are, as far as I know, completely without precedent in Welsh.

This analysis so far may give the impression that the novel is rather dry and serious, but nothing could be further from the truth. Gwynn's playful wit and eye for comedic dialogue are never far away, particularly in the first half of the novel. A favourite set-piece of Gwynn's is to have two conversations happening at once, one serious, the other comic, with characters rather implausibly misunderstanding one another, a device he deploys on two separate occasions in this novel. Another wonderful example of Gwynn's wit is this magnificent response by Olwen to Richard in Chapter VIII:

> "I was thinking that at some point he must have been associating with cultured and sophisticated people, even if he doesn't now."

> "It's quite possible," said Olwen sternly, "after all, I don't think he ever went to university."

These humorous elements are yet another element which Gwynn weaves into his whole in a naturalistic way, and though they peter out as the novel rushes towards its increasingly cataclysmic climax, they help mitigate against some of the more serious elements and prevent the more sentimental parts of the novel from veering into kitsch.

One additional aspect of Gwynn's personal biography demands mention: his personal correspondence provides ample evidence that when writing the novel he was in a period of personal religious agnosticism. Whilst he became a committed Christian in the later part of his life Gwynn's relationship with religion oscillated constantly throughout most of his adult life, back and forth from outright atheism through agnosticism to periods of fairly steady religious attendance, and even flirtations with Catholicism. Gwynn stops short of making his hero an outright atheist, though the fact the other characters treat him as one is a direct stab at the intolerant dogmatism he perceived in the religious society around him. However, Gwilym is clearly plagued by doubts, and repeatedly asks how God can permit suffering, questions the narrative leaves deliberately unanswered. Similarly, the minister's attempts to comfort the bereaved Mr. Morrus are deliberately pathetic. There are parallels to Christ in Gwilym's character arc: he spends time in the wilderness, becomes a leader of men, is betrayed by them, and finally sacrifices himself for the wellbeing of those around him. Throughout the novel it is always Gwilym's behaviour which is the most obviously Christian—indeed, he is sometimes saintly to the point of stretching credibility. In the introduction to the new Welsh edition I called this novel 'the Great Welsh Agnostic novel', and it is an apt description, for clearly these elements are of equal or even greater importance to the novel's political radicalism, and it is in this respect perhaps that the novel most obviously diverges from contemporary expectations of the novel in Welsh.

The novel has its faults of course. Gwynn is not above employing the stereotypes and conventions of the Victorian novelist, such as stock characters: we have the reformed drunk (Richard), the loving wife (Hannah), the crone with a heart of gold (Nansi). The novel uses both of the go-to elements Victorian novelists employed to stimulate interest: improbable coincidences and mysteries often deployed more for 'twist' value than because they are necessary. Does the revelation that Richard is Gwilym's father really add or change anything? The author is also happy to dip into sentimentality on occasion, in particular with Gwen bach, where any pathos the author intended to evoke is drowned in sheer schmaltz (one suspects she is a long-lost cousin of Dickens's Tiny Tim). We must also acknowledge the awkwardness of the discussion of the 'black pagans' in chapters VI-VII, though we should do so in the context of the novel's age, and with an awareness of Gwynn's long history as a critic of the British Empire and as a champion of minorities and oppressed groups of all kinds.

The above elements notwithstanding, for the most part *The Great Deed of Gwilym Bevan* is a novel which feels remarkably fresh for its age, and one suspects that if anything it will hold more appeal to audiences in 2024 than it did in 1899. The way Gwynn successfully weaves the political and philosophical elements into the narrative without them feeling shoehorned marks him out as a master of this kind of writing, and one can't help but feel that the Welsh novel in the twentieth century might have taken a very different course—and a better one—had this, and Gwynn's other novels, received more attention than they did. As it is, and despite Gwynn's stature as a poet, the novel is almost completely unknown to audiences in Wales or anywhere else. If this translation makes any difference to that, then it will have served its purpose.

Note on the Translation

This translation is based on the new Welsh edition from Melin Bapur, which in turn is based on the version which appeared in 1906 on the pages of *Y Cymro*. I have translated under the assumption that my reader has no knowledge of the Welsh language, history or culture, and accordingly have provided footnotes on occasion where I have felt such a reader might benefit from a more detailed explanation.

Throughout I have tried to reflect Gwynn's style as a writer of the Victorian era; when encountering phrases which are difficult or impossible to translate I have reproduced them either by transliterating the Welsh or leaving them in Welsh (with explanations in the footnotes). Though he provided titles for the third chapter onwards, Gwynn did not provide titles for the first two chapters of the book; for consistency I have given them titles in this translation.

In Anglicising their names (a practice Gwynn detested) the Welsh have adopted a variety of spellings; Morrus might just as easily be rendered Morris or Morus. Often a person's official name might be anglicised, like Thomas, but be referred to day-to-day by a Welsh form like Tomos. I have maintained in every circumstance the spellings as they appear in the Welsh.

Where there are verses or snatches of song in Welsh, I have left these as they were, and then provided a prose translation in brackets; those interested can thus trace the rhyme and metre of the originals.

Gwynn anticipated that his original audience understood English, and thus did not provide any explanation for phrases appearing in English (specifically, parts of the hymn *Martyrs of the Arena*, and the quotation from Ruskin in Chapter X). The biblical quotations in the original work are from the iconic translation of 1588 by William Morgan, a work of enormous significance to the development of the Welsh language; in this translation, with a single exception (on the final page, clearly noted) I have used the so-called King James version, which of course occupies an appropriately equivalent position in relation to the English language. I have not provided the book, chapter and verse for these biblical quotations, as Gwynn did not do so, simply assuming his readers would recognise the quotations. Those interested will be able to find them easily enough.

I am extremely grateful to Richard Pearce, Beatrice Pearce and Molly Newton for proof-reading the text.

Adam Pearce, Porthcawl, 2024

Adam Pearce is the general editor of Melin Bapur Books. He holds a PhD from Bangor University on the English translations of Daniel Owen, another literary giant of the Welsh language in the nineteenth century. He has previously published translations of Daniel Owen into English, and H. G. Wells into Welsh. Originally from Barry in South Wales, he now lives in Porthcawl with his family.

Chapter I.
The River

Four o'clock Sunday Morning, in July, on the Thames Embankment in London, having just awoken from a restless sleep on a hard bench, having not eaten a scrap of food for almost two days, and without a penny to his name: that was how things were for Gwilym Bevan.

The sun's early rays lit up the river, making it shine like glass; the place was relatively quiet, although a host of others much like Gwilym had spent the night there: some asleep, others staring into the clear water as if they were ready to leap into its deep embrace. Soon the policemen would come, and the unfortunates would have to go somewhere else—poverty is welcome nowhere.

Gwilym was starving, and indeed it was the painful pangs of his stomach that had woken him from his uneasy sleep. He sat up, and saw the clear river stretched out like a mirror before him. He turned to look at it, as, for a moment, his wonder at its beauty and grandeur were equal to his famine.

Gwilym stared long at the river, and whispered to himself, in Welsh:

"Oh, it's beautiful. God was so generous with nature, so—" he stopped, and presently, he whispered slowly, "but was he generous to men?"

The river flowed on without a wave to break its smooth surface, and Gwilym rose, went to the wall, and looked down at the water. The current was so smooth, so clear and pure in the sunlight: plenty of water to break his thirst, and indeed, to break his fast too—to break them both forever! And why not? He had never asked to live in such a world; he had merely found himself to be living in it. His earliest memory was of playing with other children on a riverbank in Wales. One of the other children had been angry with him about something and had sought his revenge by telling Gwilym that it was only through chance that he existed at all. The child did not understand what he had said, no doubt, and neither did Gwilym himself know what the words meant. The child was merely repeating something he'd heard said by others, older and crueller than himself.

But Gwilym came to understand. The people who raised him were not his parents. If it had ever been known, nobody had told him who his father was; he never saw his mother, as her eyes had closed forever before his own had opened for the first time. He knew nothing of his mother's story either, as she had been a stranger in the place where he had been born, and it was only through pity that a poor worker and his wife had taken him in and given him his name. But that man had died in the quarry, and his wife, her heart broken, had followed shortly after. With their deaths Gwilym had lost the only friends he possessed, for everyone else in the parish, though kind enough towards him, would say with their eyes what some of them would say to him with their mouths on occasion: that he was a child of sin.

Besides the couple who'd raised him there had been only one who had looked upon him and spoken with him differently. That man was a Curate, and an Englishman. He had come to the area to conduct services in English in a kind of missionary church. He was a man who did his best for the poor, and had taken the young orphan child of unknown parents and given him lessons. And yet, there had been a strike in the quarry, and the curate had preached a questionable sermon. He didn't stay long after that. Gwilym thus lost all his allies. He found work in the quarry, but had found that he had a desire to see the world. He had thus wondered far and made his way eventually to London. He found no golden pavements there. He had worked hard through each long day, and spent the evening hours in the libraries, but soon enough his strength had failed him, his health failed him, his employer failed him, and that beautiful summer morning, his hope was about to fail him!

Were they right after all, those people among whom he'd been raised? Was he a creature with no right to live? If so, then why live? The water below was so calm, so smooth. A feather fell from a passing seagull's wing. It danced lightly in the breeze, until it reached the surface of the water. Yes, the water was drawing him in!

Gwilym climbed onto the wall, saying to himself, "Why not?"

"What are you doing?" asked a voice in Welsh behind him, and he found himself being pulled back down. He turned his head to see not, as he had expected, a policeman, but a young woman in a nurse's uniform.

Her face was like—like a picture of the Virgin Mary he had seen in one of the city's art galleries. The thought had stuck Gwilym like a bullet, despite where he was, and he looked at the girl for some time without daring to answer her question. She asked again:

"What are you doing?"

"Well," said Gwilym, "I was going to jump; forgive me—"

"Why are you asking my forgiveness?"

"I didn't mean to startle you."

"Well," said the girl, then hesitated, and went on in a more cheerful voice, "if you don't want to startle me, then please come away from that wall, and tell me what it was that made you try to do something so awful."

The girl grabbed him by the arm and led him a few yards away from the wall.

"Now," she said, "what's the matter?"

"Ill, poor, hungry—in short, everything," said Gwilym.

"Oh, don't break your heart, you'll get better, and you'll find work to pay your way again."

"Thank you for trying to comfort me, but there's no point. Everything's been against me from the start. I have been here for four years now, but I'm not a jot better off today than when I came; in fact, I'm worse—I've lost my health."

Gwilym sat on a bench nearby and held his face in his hands.

"Now, now," said the girl, "it won't do to break your heart like that. With you being Welsh, we'll see what we can do. When did you last eat?"

"I had a piece of bread yesterday morning."

"Well, no wonder you feel so miserable. Come with me, we'll go and look for something to eat."

"No, thank you, I'd rather not," said Gwilym, looking, almost without realising, at his rags, and then at her smart and clean outfit.

She saw his glance.

"You think I wouldn't want to be seen with you?" she said. "Well, really, you shouldn't be so proud—"

"Well," said Gwilym, "if you think it's pride, I'll come with you, to show you that it isn't. Though I must admit, to tell the truth, that charity feels worse to me than dying! I'm happy to work, and to work hard, if I could have my health, and a position."

"Oh, well," said the girl, "I see you're a little proud after all, if you don't mind my saying."

"Well, maybe so," said Gwilym, "but I can't help it. I don't see why it's not every man's right to live without depending on anyone else's goodwill."

Gwilym said these words, not with bitterness or contempt, but in a tender and regretful tone, and in calling him proud the girl in turn had meant to tease him from his low spirits rather than anything else.

"What you say is true enough," said the girl, "and I hope that you don't think I'm offering you charity. I'd rather call it duty."

"Thank you for your kindness," said Gwilym, "and forgive me for saying that I do truly admire your way of doing a favour! And yet I'll come with you, and gratefully."

"Permit me to ask you a question," said the girl. "If I had been in your place, and you had been in mine, and had found me just as I found you just now: what would you have done?"

Gwilym looked up, his eyes brimming with tears, and looked deeply into the girl's eyes.

"Forgive me," he said, faltering, "you're right. But you're one in ten thousand, or more. I—I—I'll do whatever you ask."

"We'll go this way, then," said the girl, and led her poor companion through the streets to her own lodgings. She had a comfortable room and had soon prepared her poor compatriot a breakfast. Once he had acknowledged that she was right, she spoke more freely with him, which made him feel in turn that she was not deigning to do him a favour from pity, but that she genuinely wanted to help him.

"Now then," she said, as they both ate, "I'd like you to tell me your story, that is, as much of it as you'd like to share, and then we'll see what we can do."

Had someone else asked such a question of him, Gwilym would have refused. Not because he was ashamed of himself, but because he would have felt that their request was mere nosiness and curiosity. But somehow he felt he could trust this girl, and tell her everything, and he did so, much in the way his story was summarised at the start of this chapter. He told her everything except for one thing—he did not tell her that he had been an illegitimate child.

The girl listened attentively, and not without feeling the tears come to her own eyes more than once.

"Well," she said presently, "I have every sympathy for you. All I did was get bored of doing nothing, and so I became a nurse. I couldn't bear sitting idle all the time without doing anything to help anyone else, and so I came here, and I'm not the same person now that I used to be."

"The world would be a better place if more people were like you," said Gwilym, and he was about to add, "although there can't be another woman like you in the whole world," but he stopped himself. The words felt too much like empty flattery, though he sincerely believed them. He could say that about her to someone else, but to say it to her? He could almost worship her, but not praise her—praise—the way of the unprincipled courtier, the sycophant! Gwilym said nothing, and looked at the girl, gazing at her face at length. Wasn't that a face like—like what? Like the sunlight on the water had been—drawing him in and giving an impression of rest and comfort.

"You shall have to return home to Wales," said the girl, "that's what you need: this city's air is poisoning you, and you being so fragile. You've worked yourself too hard, that's the reality."

"Yes, I suppose. But there was nothing else I could do. I can't go back to Wales."

"Oh, don't upset yourself again. I'll lend you the money for the train, and you can pay me back after you've found work." Gwilym could not have refused her had he wanted to, and so he accepted the terms, and promised he would pay her back as soon as he found work. He left, and the next day, having bid the girl farewell, he returned to Wales. He would have preferred to stay in London, if only because then he might see her face sometimes, but with a heavy heart, Gwilym accepted his fate, and departed. He would never forget her, that was all! He took her name and address, which she wrote down for him. So he would know where to send the money to pay her back? Of course; and yet Gwilym kept the card on which she had written as long as he lived.

Chapter II.
The Quarry and the Choir

Some months passed, and by now Gwilym was working in Craig y Coed[*] quarry. He had, before going to Craig y Coed, earned enough to be able to return the girl the money, but he never received so much as a single word to acknowledge it. That fact pained him, yet then again, why should he have expected her to write back to him?

Fresh air and a better diet than he had enjoyed for years had brought him new strength, and though the work at Craig y Coed was hard and the pay pitiful, Gwilym's hopes were slowly being restored.

Craig y Coed quarry's owner was one Mr. Thomas Morrus, a man held in high esteem both near and far, by all accounts; and certainly worthy of respect, for Mr. Morrus was a very religious man, and something of a public figure, having worked his way up through various difficulties to reach the position in which he now found himself. He had a wife and two children, a son and a daughter; the son at university and the daughter also away from home. Some three hundred men were employed at the quarry, the majority of them conscientious and virtuous men enough. The Welsh quarryman is a generous and sociable creature, as a rule. Give him a fair enough deal, and he will work happily enough all day; he will read his newspaper during his

---

[*] *Craig y Coed:* lit. Wood Rock; often quarries would take names from nearby features, which might then disappear as they expanded.

lunch hour, or rather, each *caban*[*] will have its own reader, with the rest his eager audience. In his evenings the quarryman goes to the *seiat*,[†] or the prayer meeting, or the choir; on the Sunday he will attend chapel, without fail, and that is his week.

The quarrymen at Craig y Coed led similar enough lives to this outline. The majority lived in Treganol[‡], and as there were various other industries with branches in the town its population was some five or six thousand. Gwilym shared little with the others at the quarry, but soon enough his new colleagues had worked out that he was, to put it as they did, "someone". Although he had worked in a quarry before he found that he needed to re-learn the craft to all intents and purposes; however this only contributed to the impression that he was "more than just a quarryman".

Gwilym neither denied nor admitted these ideas his colleagues had about him, and soon enough they ceased interrogating him as he was a likeable young man; furthermore, he seemed to possess considerable knowledge on any subject which happened to arise, something else which made him someone with whom it was worth being on good terms.

Because of his studious habits, and the aforementioned knowledge, Gwilym soon enough became something of a hero among the quarrymen at Craig y Coed. However, as he did not seem to profess any particular religion, and as he would only very seldom

---

[*] *Caban*. Workers' cabins in the slate industry were a cultural institution where the men would discuss politics, philosophy, religion and literature.

[†] *Seiat*. A chapel meeting in the Calvinist Methodist church for full members of a chapel.

[‡] *Treganol*. Lit. "Middle-town"; Gwynn clearly wished the novel's setting to be non-specific.

attend either chapel or church, in short order he was given the nickname, "the Atheist". No one dared say such a thing to his face of course, but they would say it to one another nevertheless, and one or two even mentioned this to Mr. Morrus—for no other reason than concern for the young man's own wellbeing, of course. The thing that the good people of Treganol found strangest of all, however, was that despite being an "Atheist", or at least having his doubts, Gwilym nevertheless seemed to keep to the straight and narrow, living an unblemished life. There was nothing, as far as anyone knew, in his manner that suggested he might be dangerous. On the contrary, it was widely known that he was teetotal, and that he had worked hard alongside some of the town's ministers to have the judges revoke the licence of one of the area's least reputable drinking establishments. It was known also that he was a strong advocate of the evening schools, and that he had even given a whole week's wages toward the establishment of a new County School that was being built in the town. Many, indeed, all of those who wished to know more about the young stranger's past, found all these things difficult to reconcile.

They would be surprised still further one Sunday evening toward the end of Autumn. It was a beautiful evening, and as people were leaving the chapels, and walking slowly homewards along the main street, they saw about a dozen young men gathered in the middle of the town square, who presently began to sing. A good crowd had soon collected around them, for the young men were singing wonderfully. They sang a hymn or two, and then an anthem or two, and to finish they sang a piece that drove the musically-inclined quarrymen half wild, such was its power and majesty.

"That's the *Martyrs*, lad!" said one young man to another beside him, as the singers hit the first note.

"Yes," said his companion, "and they'll sing it wonderfully for you, too!"

And they did just that. Their voices were strong, clear and disciplined; they sang carefully and powerfully, and the crowd pressed against one another to listen to them:

> *Great Caesar, with our dying breath,*
> *Thus we hail thee!*
>
> *The body thou canst doom to death,*
> *Willing tools will not fail thee;*
> *But the soul shall hold fast her faith.*
> *O Caesar, with our dying breath,*
> *Thus we hail thee!*
> *Great Lord of life and death.*
>
> *See the town keeps holiday today,*
> *The circus, in festive array.*
> *Now raise a merry shout to the Gods.*
> *With cymbals clashing and trumpets blowing,*
> *Before them the stern lictor's rods.*
> *See the consuls in crimson glowing,*
> *See the pale vestal's white robes flowing,*
> *All attend till the great Caesar nods.*
>
> *And we, all amid the dread arena,*
> *Naked, defenceless, in God our sole reliance,*
> *We hear, we hear with calm defiance,*
> *The roaring lion and hyena,*
> *Soon to be our living tomb.*
>
> *Heard ye that ringing cheer?*
> *They open now the cage,*
> *And the tiger and panther in their rage,*
> *They come madly bounding along.*

> *Brethren, be strong!*
> *Lift up the heart in prayer and song!*
>
> *God of the martyr and the slave,*
> *O Christ who has triumphed over death,*
> *Come, O come, Thy suffering saints to save.*
> *Now they draw their parting breath!*
>
> *Tis the hour of joyful compensation!*
> *Hark! it greets us from eternity;*
> *Now comes the long looked for salvation,*
> *Now dawns the day of liberty.*
>
> *God of the martyr and the slave,*
> *O Christ, who has triumphed over death,*
> *Come, O come, Thy suffering saints to save.*
> *Now they draw their parting breath;*
>
> *And when the life blood is pouring,*
> *And day is darkening into night,*
> *O living God, to thee our souls are soaring*
> *And death is the dawning of endless light.**

As the singing ended with glorious power on the words "And death is the dawning of endless light", a young man climbed to the top of the steps that surrounded the lamp at the middle of the square.

"Gwilym!" whispered the quarrymen to one another when they saw who it was. His face was pale, and his lips trembled. He took off his hat and stood for a moment or

---

* Gwynn does not quote the hymn in full in his original novel, but it would likely have been more familiar to his readers, as the Treganol crowd's response suggests. The words to *The Martyrs of the Arena* are an English translation by James Stallybrass of the original French hymn by François De Rillé.

two without saying a word. Everyone waited attentively. What was he going to say?

"*And death is the dawning of endless light!*" said the young man slowly, quoting the choir's English words, "Send that light, Oh, God, ere we die!"

"Speak Welsh!" someone shouted from the crowd.

"Quiet!" said a gentleman, a stranger wearing cycling clothes who stood nearby; but the people demanded Welsh, and Gwilym changed to speak that language.

"My fellow countrymen," he said, "forgive me for addressing you in English—it was the singing in English that put me in that mind. I've been asked to say something to you on behalf of these here singing for us. They are colliers, from the South. As you know they are striking there, and there is great poverty. These men are going from place to place and singing, and are sending the donations they receive from sympathetic listeners back home to those who are suffering. Singing for a scrap of bread is hard work. I need not tell you of the circumstances that led these men to strike. There are some who say that it is they who are in the wrong, and that it's their own fault they must do this. There are few men who would starve themselves on a whim, and fewer still who'd let their wives and their young children suffer on a whim. If they are in the wrong, then they have the right at least to be called honest, and there's not a man in his right mind who can fail to sympathise with them. Can I appeal to you to show them your support? A man once said—a man whom most of you have been worshipping this evening—'A new commandment I give to you, that you love one another.' That is the greatest commandment humankind ever received—obeying it will change the world. Think about this commandment, and look at these men."

He pointed at the singers, and the crowd turned their gaze upon the young men. Gwilym climbed down, and whilst the crowd's attention was on the collection, he slipped quietly away. Only one man saw him go, and followed after him. It was a stranger, wearing cycling clothes, the one who had asked for quiet when Gwilym had spoken in English and the crowd had demanded Welsh.

Gwilym strode energetically away from the town, and quickly reached the path that crossed the fields to the sea. The stranger followed him still, but Gwilym was walking on the beach before the stranger caught him. The waves broke on the sand in a low murmur, and occasionally a deeper roar from further out to sea. Gwilym stood to listen to the sound, and whispered to himself, "And death is the dawning of endless light—light—light!"

The stranger went and stood a few steps from him, and like him, stared at the sea, listening to the murmur and the roar, still coming from afar, so strong, so constant, so deep.

"It speaks of the unimaginable, doesn't it?" said the stranger, in English.

"Yes, "answered Gwilym, turning to look at the stranger, "yes, the light disappears beyond it—"

"Ah, yes, the light; the light is life!"

The two faced one another, and the stranger extended his hand. Gwilym returned the gesture.

"Professor Eldon?" he said.

"The same. I believe we have met somewhere before now?"

"Yes, in one of your lectures in—. Perhaps you'll remember a young Welshman who was bold enough to come and ask you a question at the end of a lecture, some four or five years ago?"

"Yes, I remember it well. I'm pleased to meet you again. Thank you for your speech this evening; though I didn't understand a word of the Welsh, I think I understood the meaning."

"Oh," said Gwilym, blushing, "I wish I hadn't said anything. But I couldn't do anything else, despite myself. It was the singing that finished me. I had to do something. I just hope they don't remember who it was that spoke."

"Why? What makes you say that?"

"I don't know. Every time I do something like that—and I won't unless I can't help myself—this feeling comes over me, and I find I want to go, and be out of sight right away. I'd like to be able to talk without being seen."

"You're too meek," said the Professor.

"Oh, no, I've plenty of ambition, in my own way. There's not a man alive who doesn't like to feel he has influence, but there's something contemptible in seeking influence for its own sake—nothing but an empty ambition!"

"Ah!" said the Professor, "how much the greater men's influence would be, if they realised that."

"And yet," said Gwilym, "I can't subscribe to that either. Is everyone's ambition just empty? Regardless, the sea and the stars are better company; so great that one forgets oneself in them!"

"Indeed, they're majestic, aren't they?"

The two walked slowly back to the town, and talked late into the evening in Gwilym's lodgings, a tiny room in a tiny house on the edge of town. There was nothing in it except a table, two chairs, and four or five shelves to hold books. The only light was the weak twilight that came through the tiny window, and yet the men spoke still.

At length, the Professor announced, "Well, I must go; the people at the hotel told me they would expect my return by ten o'clock. It's gone ten already. I'm very pleased to have met you, and if I'm ever in these parts again, I shall look you up. Stick to your present course—the light will come; in the evening, perhaps, but it will come."

"Thank you very much. I'll see you back to the hotel, with your permission."

"Certainly, come, let's go." The two left in the direction of the hotel where the Professor was to spend that night. There they bade each other farewell, the learned man returning to his rooms, and the poor workman to his bleak lodgings, where he sat by the window to read. He kept reading until the failing light dipped below the distant horizon.

Chapter III.
Under Scrutiny

Gwilym's speech was the talk of the town the following week. There was a wide range of opinions concerning it, but regardless, it had clearly moved something in the people's hearts, and the colliers did better from their collection there than anywhere else in the district.

At the quarry the following Monday morning, his fellow workers' praise was so widespread that Gwilym scarcely had a moment's peace, and yet it was with a heavy heart that he listened to them. What was it that he had done to receive such praise? Had he not done it merely by instinct, as if in a dream? And what good had it done, anyway, to be spoken of in such terms? He endeavoured to persuade his comrades to leave the thing alone, but in vain. They were passionate men, and quick to make a hero of one who had pleased them.

But it was not long before Gwilym had to endure more than just praise. Others had heard his speech, men not possessed of the quarrymen's weaknesses, nor their virtues. These were not the kind of men who share their feelings by talking about them. They had an alternative outlet: the press. Almost everyone in Treganol received a certain weekly newspaper, and when it arrived in the town towards the end of that week, its readers found within it a letter concerning Gwilym's speech, or rather, concerning the one who had delivered it.

The letter, addressed to "The Editor, *Flame of Freedom*", read as follows:

"SIR,—

I know that the morals and religion of our country are of sufficient concern to you, such that you will permit me to draw your readers' attention to a matter of great importance to all who love our country's wellbeing, and its soul.

Last Sunday evening, as I was walking along the road from the chapel, my thoughts engaged in a deep contemplation of those great truths which had been spoken therein, I heard the sound of singing on the square. I took them to be a flock of Sabbath-breakers, and quietly I prayed for myself, 'Turn away mine eyes from beholding vanity.' Yet swiftly I was given to believe that they were singing some of Wales's ancient, sacred hymns, and so went to see who they were. I saw soon enough that they were colliers, from the South. Now, far be it from me to say anything against the colliers, whom we know are suffering at present; no, on the contrary, I sympathise with them from the bottom of my heart, and the depths of my soul. And yet, I would ask, whether it is appropriate for them to wander the land thus, singing, on the Lord's Day? Are the other six days not enough, without disturbing the peace of the Sabbath?

Yet that is not all to which I would draw attention. When the men finished singing, a young man ascended the steps of the great lamp-post in the middle of the square, and addressed the people. I have nothing against the young man personally, yet feel I should draw attention to the matter, that he might not believe himself to be wise. It was in English that he began his speech, a language of which his knowledge, without doubt, will have been the medium through which he has received a great many of these wild ideas of his. He made reference to our duty to love one another, and in doing so perverted the Lord Jesus's commandment to his own purpose. The speech had the intended effect on the people, and I understand that a great collection was had. Yet who, in truth, is this man who would teach the believers of Treganol their duty? If I have heard correctly, he is no more than an Atheist, or an Agnostic, and has no faith in Him to whom he was referring when commanding us to love one another. Furthermore, after he had finished speaking, the young man was seen walking off quickly, and later on was seen in the company of one of those half-civilised foreigners who come to our country to profane the Sabbath by riding around on their wheeled steeds! Are these the kinds of men who are to teach the believers of Treganol their duty? Let the reader answer.

Yours, in prayer,
A MINISTER."

By that night there was not a soul in Treganol who had not either read the letter nor heard its contents shared, and they were much disturbed. The quarrymen were ready to defend their colleague to a man; indeed, there is reason to suspect that some of them may even have sworn and cursed quite fiercely when they read the letter, or heard it read. Others—shopkeepers, and people who lived in relative comfort—read the epistle with serious faces, and some began to feel guilty at having donated a penny or two to the young men who had sung in the street on a Sunday evening.

The letter even drew the attention of the lawyers—at least, it drew the attention of one of them, none other than Mr. Jenkin Jeffreys, a man commonly referred to locally as the Lager Lawyer. Mr. Jenkin Jeffreys was not over-burdened with work, and did not concern himself greatly with how he obtained that work which he could get. He had been eagerly awaiting the delivery of the *Flame of Freedom* to his office, and no sooner had it been brought in by the boy who served as his clerk, messenger and general dogsbody than Mr. Jeffreys began reading carefully, beginning at the beginning and leaving no column unread. He read the stories from the courts with great care, but, judging by the look on his face, there was nothing there of particular interest to Mr. Jeffreys. Presently he reached those columns which featured the "letters to the editor." He once more paid close attention to these, and found there a short letter concerning "Temperance in Glyn." This letter included the words,

"I saw the owner of the largest alehouse in the village carrying a dozen barrels up from the railway station on Saturday evening. There must be a great quantity of beer consumed in the locality, and why had the beer to be moved on the Saturday evening?"

Mr. Jeffreys smiled, and with great relish, underlined these words, before going on to read the letter from the "Minister." Then he rang the bell to summon the aforementioned boy.

"Take down a letter or two for me, boy," said Mr. Jeffreys. The boy made ready to take the dictation, and Mr. Jeffreys began.

The first was "To Mr. John Jones, Fox Inn, Glyn." In brief, it noted that Mr. Jeffreys's attention had been drawn to the fact that the *Flame*, on such-and-such a date, had included letters referring to Mr. John Jones in such a way that might lead the public to believe that Mr. Jones was in the habit of selling beer illegally on Sundays. Such a suggestion was, Mr. Jeffreys believed, both impudent and malicious, and certain to cause harm to Mr. Jones's business; such that he felt it his duty to draw Mr. Jones's attention to the matter.

"One minute," said Mr. Jeffreys to the boy, "who was the young man who gave the speech on the square when those men were singing?"

"Gwilym Bevan," said the boy.

"Ah yes. Wait a minute—who is Gwilym Bevan?"

"He's a quarryman sir, works in Craig y Coed."

"Oh yes," said Mr. Jeffreys, who then dictated a second letter, this one to send to Gwilym, to the effect that he had noticed that the *Flame* featured letters which, without doubt, were slanderous to Gwilym's character. Mr. Jeffreys felt, or so he wrote, that it was high time a stop was put to such letters as these, which were written under false names by individuals claiming to be religious in order merely to stain the character of honest and respectable people.

In truth, the effect the letter from the "Minister" had on the people of Treganol was not far removed from that described by Mr. Jeffreys. In the following issue of the *Flame*, clarifications were published to explain the meaning of the letter concerning "Temperance in Glyn," alongside an apology to Mr. John Jones, Fox Inn, which brought a satisfied smile to the lips of Mr. Jeffreys. However, he was far less satisfied when he saw the following words, in the form of another letter to the editor:

"SIR,—

I am neither an Atheist nor Agnostic. It was slanderous to call the gentleman I spoke with a half-civilized foreigner and Sabbath-breaker.

Yours sincerely,
GWILYM BEVAN.

"Why, the fool should let me do the work for him!" said Mr. Jeffreys to himself.

The "Minister" was not pleased however, and though he did not send another letter to the Flame, he instead drew the attention of Mr. Morrus to the matter.

Mr. Morrus was a deacon in the chapel where the Reverend Calfin Jones, the letter's author, was minister, and thus it was natural enough that a respectable man would bring the matter to his attention. To give the Reverend Calfin Jones his due, he did not mean Gwilym any harm, for though he was a narrow-minded and prejudiced man, and thus liable to persecute others, he was not, despite this, in any way vengeful or cruel by nature. Accordingly, his only action was to draw Mr. Morrus's attention to the fact that it was dangerous for a young man like Gwilym Bevan to mislead the young men of their church, among whom, he understood, there was considerable sympathy with Gwilym on this matter; indeed, he had heard that some of the young men had been quite vocal in encouraging him to write the letter to the newspaper.

"Something like this could start to foster free thinking amongst these youths, you see, Mr. Morrus," said the Reverend, "and it's our duty to be very careful."

"True enough," responded Mr. Morrus, "but under the circumstances, it's very difficult to do anything, you see. I have men working in the quarry who lead loose and prodigal lives, and do so openly. It would please me greatly if I could offer employment only to men of virtue, but I cannot do so, despite my best efforts. As far as I can tell, this boy sticks to the straight and narrow; indeed, the men think the world of him, and not without good reason, from what I hear; and if I were to turn him away it would do more harm than good, not only to myself, but to our great cause here, for circumstances force me to give work to some who are much worse than he is, and there would be all sorts of trouble for me, professionally, if I turned him away."

"Of course, I see the difficulty. But perhaps you could speak with him? It's strange that a boy like him, who lives a sober and steady life, and who reads so much, should so completely neglect the means of grace. I worry that he has been to England—they say he can speak English as well as he speaks Welsh, or even better—and that he has picked up some wild ideas; and it's just intolerable that the seeds of heathenism might be sown thus amongst our young people, Mr. Morrus, and for us to do nothing to stop this terrible evil!"

"Yes, indeed," said Mr. Morrus, "I'll speak with the boy the first chance I get. But there's nothing I can do besides that, remember."

However, Mr. Morrus was not altogether excellent at remembering his promises, and before he remembered, or had a chance to speak to Gwilym, other events took place which drew the attention of Mr. Morrus to such a degree that he lost all memory of his promise to Mr. Calfin Jones.

The same evening as this conversation between the Rev. Calfin Jones and Mr. Morrus, a letter addressed to Mr. Morrus arrived from London to inform him that his daughter had been taken dangerously ill. Mr. Morrus read the letter with a heavy heart, and then called for his wife.

"Hannah," he said, "now I don't wish to frighten you, but—"

"Oh, what's happened, what is it?"

"You mustn't take alarm," said Mr. Morrus, "but Olwen has been taken ill, and—"

"Oh! Oh!"

Mrs. Morrus threw herself onto a nearby chaise-loungue, wailing and sighing uncontrollably.

"Oh, this is what I said would happen! Oh, why did she insist on going away, to that awful old London, to the midst of every danger and temptation, and to become a nurse, of all things, amongst wretches of all sorts, and afflictions of every kind. Oh, what else was to be expected? Oh, what shall I do, what shall I do?"

"Don't take on so," said Mr. Morrus tenderly. "She isn't as bad as all that—at least, the doctor says that the danger is over now, and that she'll be able to come home within a few days. It will do her good, more than likely, and will clear some of those wild ideas from her head."

"Oh, dear Olwen, when will she come home?" wailed Mrs. Morrus, and Mr. Morrus had his hands full for some time trying to comfort his wife.

By the end of the week Olwen had returned. She was pale and thin, but had already begun to improve, and was expected to make a full recovery soon enough in the fresh mountain air, as she was by nature a strong and healthy young woman.

Chapter IV.
In Danger

The gossip about Olwen Morrus's illness, and her return home, spread quickly; and eventually reached Gwilym's ears. He and his partners were eating their midday meal in the *caban* when the talk turned to Mr. Morrus.

"His daughter's come home ill, hasn't she?" said one of the men.

"That's what I heard," said another. "Say, where was she, and what was she doing there?"

"Nobody rightly knew, until just now;" said the third. "Everyone was under the impression that she had gone away travelling, and she had been gone a long time, and now the story's come out. Turns out she was a nurse in London—"

"What—what did you say her name was?" said Gwilym, his heart beating like a hammer in his chest.

"Olwen," said one of the men, "and Olwen was a nice girl, she was. Hopefully she'll get better—she's the best of that family, and by a long way too."

The news had come so suddenly that Gwilym could scarcely believe it. It was Mr. Morrus's daughter, after all, who had saved his life that Sunday morning months ago on the Thames Embankment, and who had lent him the money to come home to Wales! He wondered why he had not come to learn of it earlier. She had not told him from which part of Wales she had come, and he had not asked; and though he had heard mention once or twice that Mr. Morrus had a son and a daughter he had never heard anything to suggest that it was Mr. Morrus's daughter who had saved him. And yet, it still seemed strange somehow that he had not known.

Gwilym went back to work, but his mind wandered to that face he had seen on the Thames Embankment, and then from there to the picture he had seen of the Madonna in one of the galleries in London. He remembered the conversation they had had that memorable Sunday morning when he had almost jumped into the river and put an end to his life. Would he see her again? Would she like to see him again? Did she remember anything about him, besides the fact she had pitied him, and saved him? Gwilym found himself stopping frequently to think such thoughts, and more than once his colleagues asked him what the matter was.

Some weeks went by, and Olwen's health improved, but more slowly than had been expected. Gwilym made enquiries every day, and somehow or other managed to find out how she was without arousing suspicion. Spring came, and Olwen had yet to leave the house, but when a week or two of glorious weather came at the end of February, the doctor announced that she could take a stroll, which reached Gwilym's ears one morning as he walked to his work. His heart leaped with joy, and perhaps with hope too, for he dreamed of seeing her face and hearing her voice once again, when he was asleep and awake. He feared meeting her, and yet longed to see her. As a memory, he loved her, but as a real woman, he worshipped her.

On Saturdays the quarrymen would finish their work at midday, and for some weeks now they had been meeting after work to discuss and organise a deposition to the owner for better terms. A number of new workers had come to the quarry in recent months, and many of these felt far stronger than the old hands did regarding their conditions. Most of the older workers had been raised in the quarry, as it were: they had worked ever since they were boys, and far less quick to act than their younger colleagues. The meetings took place every Saturday however, and the feeling grew ever deeper amongst those employed at Craig y Coed that they were being exploited. Naturally enough, the quarrymen wished to elect their leaders in this matter from the most capable amongst them, and soon enough Gwilym's service was called for in the meetings. He was very reluctant to act, however. He had spoken at one meeting before, and had had such an influence on the men on that occasion that they had insisted on acting immediately, giving no thought whatsoever to the consequences. Ever since then Gwilym had firmly refused any involvement in the campaign. He gave notice that he was perfectly willing to agree to whatever was decided, but that as he was one of the newest workers in the quarry, and because that fact could damage their cause if he were elected their leader, he would continue to refuse all nominations and all requests.

Things went from bad to worse, the rock being so poor that even the best men in the quarry, however hard they worked, struggled to earn enough to keep body and soul together,[*] and every personal application to Mr. Morrus for better terms fell on deaf ears.

One Saturday afternoon, towards the end of February, a large meeting was planned in which a course of action was to be decided. Someone had let it be known that Gwilym would speak. This was done without his knowledge or agreement, and against his wishes; and when various of his colleagues mentioned that they

---

[*] As in many industries during the nineteenth century, workers in the slate quarries were paid piecemeal, not by the hours they worked. The difference between good and poor rock was therefore a significant factor in a quarry worker's income.

looked forward to hearing him speak at the meeting in the Old Quarry that afternoon, he answered them, "It's a shame I won't be there, then."

Nevertheless, after his meal, Gwilym set off for the quarry; as in truth, he was refusing to accept the leadership of the cause despite himself. He believed the workers' cause to be inherently just, as if his own interests were completely separate; indeed, he had given no thought to himself. And yet, he knew what would happen if he dared to lead the people. He had seen plenty of evidence that their cause would be better served the less he was involved. Turning these things over and over in his head, Gwilym walked slowly towards the meeting-place. It was an unusually clear and pleasant afternoon; the sun shone hotly, the breeze was gentle, the grass a deep green, and the cloudless sky was blue. Gwilym was prone to a sort of superstition at times, and on more than one occasion, especially when in a quandary, he had felt himself guided by a kind of blind instinct, like a man, his eyes closed, walking towards a precipice. This feeling came upon him once more that afternoon as he made his way towards the Old Quarry. He turned aside from the path, and crossed the fields towards the mountains and the vast moorland—he could not say why, only that he felt he must. Crossing a slope some quarter mile from the Old Quarry, he heard singing. The workers were opening their meeting with a hymn. Gwilym turned to listen, and heard the words clearly:

> *"O, Arglwydd Dduw Rhagluniaeth*
> *Ac Iachawdwriaeth dyn,*
> *Tydi sy'n llywodraethu*
> *Y byd a'r nef dy Hun!"*

(Oh, Lord God of Providence
And Man's Salvation
It is you that governs
The world and heaven!)

A gust of wind blew, and he heard nothing of the second half of the verse. He turned and carried on his way, whispering, "And perhaps so, after all!"

He wandered deep into the mountains and sat on a mossy rock to watch the sheep grazing about him, calmly, at their leisure. There was nothing to alarm or worry them, and they had plenty of food. A lark rose up from the moor, ever higher into the blue sky. The bird sang with joyous abandon; its heart held neither concern or worry.

"And what is man—"

Before he could finish whispering his thought, he heard a cry of despair. It had come from the mountains, and was neither gull nor lapwing nor any bird. It was a cry of pain, pain and a human heart despairing. Where was it coming from? Gwilym listened. The cry again, from the lonely crags above, down from the distance, becoming little more than a sigh on the vast moor. Someone was in pain or in danger, or both.

Gwilym set off to climb the rocks, hearing the cry repeated now and again, but weaker each time. Eventually he reached a flat ledge, about ten yards across, beneath a steep crag of great height. On a narrow step a short distance from the top of the crag, gripping a slender tree that was growing from a cleft in the rock, he saw a woman. He did not want to shout for fear of frightening her, and by doing so, causing her to let go and fall. And yet he wanted to let her know that help was at hand, lest she lose heart and let go before he could reach her. As he was in this quandary, and searching for a way to climb up to her, the woman turned her head and saw him.

"Oh, help!" she cried.

"Wrap your clothes about the tree," answered Gwilym, "I'll climb up to you."

He spotted a route up to her, steep and narrow, yet easy enough to climb if one held onto the sharp rocks. Keeping his gaze fixed on the women high above him, he climbed up. Once or twice he felt faint, yet kept on climbing without once looking down. He came within some three yards of the woman, and steadied himself by pressing his hand into a cleft. The woman looked down, and Gwilym looked up. She gave a cry of surprise, and he felt his heart beat with a frenzy. There was the face he had seen that Sunday morning by the Thames!

Putting his hands and feet on the holds and pushing them into the clefts, Gwilym scrambled up, one foot at a time, until his head was level with the step upon which the woman stood. Another foot, and she would be safe— and then Gwilym felt the rock loosen and give way beneath his foot, slowly, but slipping lower and lower. He had only one chance. He could save himself by grabbing the girl's foot. And drag her down with him to the depths, no doubt! No, if he was to fall, he would do so alone. His foot slipped ever further. Any moment, he expected, his foot would lose his grip and he would fall down, down, never to get up again. The rock slipped ever lower; the next moment some tons of rock perhaps would cast him down. His stomach turned, then suddenly, he found his foot on solid rock again.

His foot had slipped into a cleft that got narrower lower down, such that he had stopped slipping once it was narrow enough to hold him.

Hope sprang up in him as he realised this, and he began climbing once more, with greater care. He felt his strength failing and his grip weakening, but still up he went, and with one final effort was able to grab hold of the trunk onto which the girl had held and drag himself up onto the ledge beside her.

Olwen offered him her hand, small, thin, and pale. He held onto it with his own rough, calloused hand. Holding each others' hands, the two stood for a moment in silence. Olwen spoke first.

"I don't know how to thank you," she said, "forgive me that I can't thank you enough; but I am pleased to see you!"

"Don't you worry about gratitude," said Gwilym, "I'll never repay my debt to you, but thank God I came up here today!"

"So you work around here now?"

"Yes, I work in the quarry at Craig y Coed."

"I thought you had completely forgotten me."

"Oh, don't say that. I would have come to see you weeks ago, had I thought that would please you."

"But you never answered my letter."

"What letter?"

"But I wrote to you, after you sent the money back to me, and I asked you to let me know how you were getting on. I never got a reply."

"I never got the letter. I must have come here before it arrived, and it must have missed me and been lost."

"Never mind that now. Here we are meeting each other again, and under such strange circumstances."

"Indeed. It feels like fate—something was pulling me this way today; I felt like I had to come."

"And something was pulling me along the Embankment that Sunday morning, despite myself."

The two fell silent, staring at each other for some time.

"How did you get to such a dangerous place today?" Gwilym asked eventually.

"Oh, I can hardly say. The doctor kept insisting I not go out, but at the start of the week he said I could go out for a walk. I longed to go out, far out, into the mountains, to the clifftops, alone, with no-one else around me. My mother wouldn't let me go anywhere far or alone, but today I got my chance. Soon enough I was making my way toward the mountain, and climbing and climbing until I reached the top of this crag. The sun was reflected in the sea, like it was glass, and the breeze was playing like living waves all around me. I went to stand near the edge, like I used to years ago, by the precipice. But I'd forgotten that I'd been fit and healthy back then. When I looked down to the depths below my head felt giddy, and I slipped, and fell, over the edge! I was lucky to land with my feet where you found me, and able to grab hold of that tree, or I would be at the bottom now."

"God forbid!" said Gwilym, quivering all over. "Perhaps it would be best not to go so close to the edge again!"

"Quite so; the depths always draw one to them."

"They do," answered Gwilym, looking long into the depths of her blue eyes, without saying anything.

They set off back down from the crag along the sheep-tracks, reaching the town as night began to fall.

"You must come with me so that my mother and father can thank you," said Olwen.

"No," said Gwilym, "I would rather not, thank you. I would rather you didn't tell them anything about me."

"Whatever for?"

"Well, I'll have to tell you some other time, perhaps."

There was something deep and serious in his voice.

"Are you sure?" asked Olwen.

"Yes, absolutely sure."

"Alright, I won't tell anyone anything about it. Good night, and—thank you." She held out her delicate, white hand to him, and he kissed it.

"Good night," he said, turning away. Olwen watched him until he disappeared from view. Then she sighed, and went inside.

Chapter V.
Through a Child's Hand

Gwilym walked slowly back to his lodgings, turning over the day's events in his head. Had it been fate, or mere accident? Notwithstanding the aforementioned state to which he was prone, Gwilym was not a superstitious man at all by nature. And yet he felt that life was full of strange, inexplicable things. Was there an invisible hand at work in all the circumstances of a man's life? Was there some truth in the old religions' teachings after all? Was mankind merely playing with truths, without really understanding them, and would some Great Mind come that could make sense of the madness, and put things in order, bringing light to the darkness which people called "an enlightened age"? How his heart longed that that should be so!

When a man thinks of such things, one cannot expect him to notice everything around him. Far more likely that he will walk headlong into whatever obstacles might happen to be in his path, or indeed, over a precipice. Though the mind can see far, it can be so blind to those things which are under its own nose; and the mind which sees furthest is often that whose own eyes are as if they are shut.

The street was busy with people, many of them inebriated, wandering here and there like ants, though without anything of the ants' order or purpose. Gwilym walked among them without noticing anyone, and was about to turn into the small, insignificant street where his lodgings were when one of his fellow workers stopped him.

"Gwilym," said the quarryman, "what were you playing at today?"

"What do you mean?" said Gwilym, slowly disentangling himself from his thoughts.

"You missed the meeting, and everyone was there waiting for you."

"Well, I never promised I would come. In fact I'm fairly certain I let it be known that I wouldn't be coming at all."

"Maybe you did, but nobody thought you were being serious. Everyone was waiting for you: the chairman even called for you to stand!"

"Well, as grateful as I am to you all for placing so much faith in me, it would be much better for you to choose someone else, older and more experienced than myself."

"Well that's what you say. But you should do what the majority want. Apart from that, and I'll tell you this now, as a friend: the men will think that you're a coward, or that you're currying favour with the bosses."

"What! Currying favour—well, to show them that I'm neither cowardly nor currying anyone's favour, let them decide whatever they want, and I'll stand with them, whatever it is they decide. I know what suffering means as well, if not better, than any of them; I'm not afraid of scorn nor am I looking for anyone's approval. But despair is an awful thing!"

The quarryman went on his way. He had understood that Gwilym was ready to "stand with them," and no more than that. Whatever Gwilym had meant when speaking of despair, he had not understood.

Gwilym continued on his way, and turned into a house in the same street as his own lodgings. It was a tiny, suffocating little place, with only the occasional piece of furniture, and yet it was clean. In the corner by the fireplace sat a man, about thirty-five years old. He had a clean, amiable face, but he was pale and bruised, and coughed pitifully as Gwilym came in. On the floor by the fireside sat two small boys, one about four, the other about two years old. They played quietly, their manner strangely mature, with a small piece of string tied to a ball of rags.

"Well, Joseff, you rogue, are you feeling any better tonight?" asked Gwilym.

"Not really," said Joseff Tomos, for that was his name; "I've been poorly again, this cough has been terrible today, though it's a little better now. Sit yourself down, Gwilym."

Gwilym sat down on a chair opposite Joseff, and as he did so, a young woman came in, a little girl, about six years old, holding her hand.

"And how's the young lady this evening, Mrs. Tomos?" said Gwilym.

"Still not right," said Mrs. Tomos, "the doctor says she's very weak, but that with care, she should pull through."

"Oh, that's good to hear," said Gwilym cheerfully. "Up you get, Gwen bach[*]," he said, reaching out his arms to receive the child.

The little girl stretched out her feeble arms towards him, and when he took her onto his lap, she looked him playfully in the eye, and said,

"Da![†]"

"Well, how is Gwen bach tonight?"

"Gwen bach sick," said the child, "tada[‡] sick too. Gwen bach going to die."

---

[*] *Bach.* Little; a common term of endearment for a child. Adjectives usually come after nouns in Welsh so Gwen Bach is "little Gwen".

[†] *Da.* Good.

[‡] *Tada.* Father. It is believed that the word 'Dad' in English may be derived from Welsh.

"Oh, no," said Gwilym, the tears brimming from his eyes despite himself, "Gwen bach will get better, and go out to play and collect flowers again when it's fine again outside. Gwen bach can come out with me tomorrow, to see the trees and mountains?"

"Oh! Yes, trees and big, big mountains, and sun too. Gwen bach can't walk far, far!"

"Oh, don't worry, we'll carry Gwen bach far, far to see the trees and the big, big mountains, and the little birds, and the sea, and the sun too."

The child clapped her little hands in delight, whispering "and sun too!" in excitement; and then, looking at Gwilym, she wrapped her tiny arms around his neck and kissed him. She then rested her head and its yellow curls on his chest with every indication of contentment as she thought of the trees and the big, big mountains, and the sun.

There was a knock at the door, and Mrs. Tomos went to open it. A man came in, and asked in a coarse, uncaring voice:

"Well, how are we this evening? Have you the rent ready?"

Joseff put his hand in his pocket and took out a half crown, and handed it to his wife. The little girl saw the half crown and began to cry quietly, hiding her pretty little face in Gwilym's coat.

"What's the matter with Gwen bach now then?" asked Gwilym.

The little girl let out a great sigh.

"Tada's giving Gwen bach's money to that horrible old man!" she said.

"Oh, we'll get the better of the horrible old man," said Gwilym, taking a half crown from his wallet. "Here's some money for Gwen bach in exchange. Here you go, Gwen bach to keep it a secret and not show anyone!"

The little girl smiled a smile worth all the half crowns in the world, truly, and the other half too, and pressed the coin to her chest. Gwilym knew full well that that half crown would feed the whole family the next day, and that her parents would take great joy from finding it, its little owner asleep, and so find her also a source of joy. The child was the medium for the gift: receiving it would be no shame for her, a gift to her would not be charity, alms, beggary, or that insult to human dignity which the world deigns to call kindness!

The little one slept in her friend's arms, still clutching the half crown tightly in her little hand which was not yet of sufficient size to close around it. Her father and mother came in.

"Oh, she's asleep," said she; "give her to me, Gwilym." She took the child from him, and the coin fell to the floor.

"Oh, Gwilym, really, you mustn't," said Mrs. Tomos, "you're much too—"

"Yes, you are, this won't do, Gwilym," said Joseff, picking up the coin and holding it out to Gwilym.

"Keep it, for her sake," said Gwilym awkwardly, "otherwise she'll be upset to wake up and find it gone—"

"But, there's no need—"

"No, give it to her, she was so pleased to have it. Anyway, I shall have to be off. It's a cold night again. Good night, Mrs. Tomos. Good night, all of you. It's getting late, I must be getting on, good night."

Even before he'd said the last "good night", Gwilym was crossing the threshold, and without waiting another second set off quickly towards the countryside.

No doubt it was just a coincidence that he wandered out past Bryn y Graig, the home of Mr. Morrus.

Bryn y Graig was a beautiful house, in a pleasant setting on the edge of town. It had a flat lawn in front, trees around it, and a large garden behind, as well as a yard, stables and other outbuildings attached.

As Gwilym passed it a door opened in the garden wall, and someone came out to meet him.

"Miss Morrus! You shouldn't be out this time of night—it's so cold!"

"Yes," said Olwen, for it was she, "but I would rather be out, and indeed I believe it is healthier for me to be out than to be indoors this evening."

Gwilym was about to ask why that might be, but he resisted the urge, and instead simply said, "Well, really, the cold air will be bad for you."

"Not half as bad as the air in that house," said Olwen scornfully. "Are you going for a walk? Can I come with you?"

Had he spoken his mind that moment Gwilym would have answered that nothing in the world would give him greater pleasure, but instead he said, "Of course, you needn't ask, but really, it's a risk for you to be out."

"Good Lord!" said Olwen, "you can't possibly be such a dangerous creature that you pose a risk to me on a walk. Don't worry, we won't go climbing again tonight."

Olwen laughed, and Gwilym smiled, though neither of them really felt like either laughing or smiling.

"That's not what I meant," said Gwilym, "I meant only that it's so cold, and—well, we're not in London and surrounded by strangers anymore, you know."

"Well," said Olwen, with a measure of something like bitterness in her voice, "should we be more hypocritical here than in London?"

"Forgive me, but you know what I mean."

The two walked along the lane from the main road, which led up to one of the hill farms.

"Let me tell you why I wanted to come out," said Olwen. "The Reverend Calfin Jones popped by. I can't stand the man at the best of times. Well, I was reading a new novel, and there's him asking me, sincerely enough, what it was I was reading. Of course, I told him. Oh, what a treat for you to have seen his face! Up went his hands, with heavenly outrage, and you never saw anyone look so much like a glass of *glastwr*[*]. 'I'm shocked, Miss Morrus' says he, 'to find you reading such books,[†] and you so recently recovered from ill health.' To tell you the truth, I was so disrespectful as to even laugh at him, I had to—I couldn't help myself—but then when he said that he didn't know what to think of young people with a good education turning to read such literature, I lost my temper with him, and said to him: 'If you'd had a good education yourself, then you would read them too, Mr. Jones. There's more Christianity in this book than one hears from the pulpit in a whole year.' And that was it. Of course my mother and father leapt to his defence. I'm not in the habit of quarrelling with them, but somehow I just couldn't help it, and in the end I had to get up and leave them all and come outside. I suppose I'm terribly bad. I don't doubt for a moment that they haven't got the best intentions, but why on earth can't *they* think that same thing about someone else? That's what drives me so wild!"

"They just can't, I suppose," said Gwilym, "at least, that's the most sympathetic interpretation I can think of."

"I'm afraid you're of a more sympathetic nature than myself, I think. Forgive me for bothering you with such nonsense, but somehow, after what happened, I feel like I can tell you, and a little sympathy helps, even for a "wild and wanton girl", as my father called me. I can put up with my father or mother saying things like that to me well

---

[*] Glastwr. Watered-down milk.
[†] See the introduction for a description of the antipathy towards novels in some religious circles.

enough, though it's a great effort at times; but when that wretched minister called me wanton too, I had to come out for fresh air, and was grateful for it!"

"It must have been hard to endure, but really, he's not worth your attention, you know. He called me an atheist—"

"What?"

Gwilym told the story of the correspondence in the Flame, whilst Olwen listened with interest.

"You know what," she said, when Gwilym had finished, "you've got tremendous patience!"

"Maybe so, but what use is getting involved? It'll make no difference in the end—"

"There you go again, you're always being fatalistic. Why don't you try expecting a little more from people?"

"Ah!" said Gwilym, "I know I can be a bit cynical, but it's impossible not to be, when you live without hope."

"Without hope," said Olwen. "Without hope for what?"

"For anything."

A great, inescapable wave of gloom came over Gwilym. He fought hard against it, but in vain. He rested his arms on the gate, and his head on his arms, and was silent.

They both stood there for a moment, and Gwilym was still. Olwen took hold of his arm.

"Gwilym," she said, "look here."

Gwilym felt a warm blush rising to his face, and was angry at himself for sharing his feelings as he had done, but he looked up, and at the girl, his heart beating quickly to hear her call him by his name for the first time.

"Gwilym," she said, "you mustn't think like that. "You—you—"

Like a bullet from a gun, someone appeared suddenly leaping over the gate, and ran straight past them without saying a word.

Chapter VI.
Charitable Words

The unrest among the quarry workers at Craig y Coed was growing, and it had now come to the attention of the *Flame* that the men were buckling under the difficult conditions of their work. About a fortnight after the Saturday when Gwilym had rescued Olwen, the *Flame* informed its readers that the workers at Craig y Coed had held a meeting "last Saturday" to consider the situation. The *Flame* did not report on the outcome of the meeting, though there was a hefty column of reportage under the title "*Craig y Coed Quarry.*" In order, one assumes, that nobody might assume that the editor, or the typsetter, or the message boy had written the column, the article had been signed "Correspondent". The correspondent in question began by explaining where Treganol was, a fact which was surely as familiar to most of the paper's readers as it was to the correspondent, especially the several hundred of them who lived there. Next, the correspondent had explained where Craig y Coed Quarry was, when it had been opened and by whom, and other such details, before describing at some length his views on the slate industry in general, enough to make it clear it was a subject about which he knew nothing, and then, having expressed his view that the majority of the workers at Craig y Coed were "honest, hard-working men, constant when it came to the means of grace, and many of them regular subscribers to the *Flame*,"; he concluded his article thus: "We understand that the quarrymen are seeking improved working conditions, and a meeting was held last week to consider the situation."

It was for want of further news that the "correspondent" had provided so little of it, for the quarrymen had held several meetings since "last Saturday", as the correspondent had put it, and had also appointed a committee to act on their behalf. The monthly salaries were paid on the first Friday in March, and it had been a poorer month than ever before. By the Saturday, many of the quarrymen were agitating for action from the committee, which was deep in consideration. They met on the Saturday evening, but no action was decided upon without further consultation at a general meeting of all the men.

Mr. Morrus had received word of what was going on in the quarry, and felt considerable unease, though he had not the slightest fear of trouble. He was in his office in the town—for he had an office in town in addition to the one at the quarry—contemplating what he had heard, when a knock came at the door.

"Come in," said Mr. Morrus, and in came Miss Gruffydd and Miss Morgan, two unmarried women of the sort sometimes referred to as "spinsters", who were well-known for their contributions to missionary work overseas.

"Good evening, ladies," said Mr. Morrus, "do come in. What is it that has brought the two of you out on such a cold and unpleasant night?"

"Oh," said Miss Gruffydd, "we have called by, Mr. Morrus, to collect for the Foreign Mission. You are of the same class as Miss Morgan and myself, and we had thought we would find you in if we called by around this time, sir."

"Ah, yes, I see," said Mr. Morrus, "I must say, there's no beating you for fundraising. Here now, how much is it that I usually give you?"

Before either of the ladies had had time to answer, a fairly heavy knock came at the door again, and, as was his habit, Mr. Morrus called out, "come in." It's quite doubtful that he would have done so had he known who was there, yet as he did, Mr. Morrus had only himself to blame when he saw Foul Mouthed Nansi come in.

Nansi was a poor old woman who lived on charity, which she would receive, as often as not, because people were afraid of her foul mouth, which she was certain to let loose on any who refused her charity. Nansi's mouth was, indeed, foul, but many, even those who had been on the receiving end of her worst insults, could affirm that her mouth was the worst thing about her. Mr. Morrus knew well enough that it would not do to behave to Nansi as he might to any other beggar, and for this reason his only response to her appearance was to give her a hostile look when she came in.

"Begging your pardon, sir, for disturbing you," said Nansi, "but I'm hard up, me, sir—"

"I shall speak to you in one moment, Nansi," said Mr. Morrus, but he did not dare to tell the old woman to go back out to wait.

"How much do I usually donate, did you say, Miss Morgan?"

"Ten pounds, sir," said Miss Morgan, "you are always the first on our list."

"Ten pounds!" said Nansi to herself, "Glory be! What for, I wonder?"

"Well, well," said Mr. Morrus, "I suppose you won't accept any less this time again, though business is very slack, almost nothing going in fact, though it's a man's duty to give to the best of causes."

"It is," said Miss Gruffydd, "did you read the story of that pagan who went to the missionary, Mr. Morrus? You didn't? Well, you should do. It's enough to break your heart to read how the poor creature asked the missionary if God was the captain of the soldiers of our country, and was it him that let them do just what they wanted. Such ignorance and darkness!"

"Yes, indeed, think of it," said Miss Morgan, "asking if God was the captain of the soldiers of this country, and whether he was fond of whisky!"

"Yes," said Mr. Morrus, "of all good causes, I know of none worthier than the Foreign Mission. Put me down for ten pounds. Which one of you two is treasurer?"

Miss Gruffydd informed him that she was treasurer, and once Miss Morgan had written Mr. Morrus's name in the book, and Mr. Morrus had transferred ten pounds to the possession of Miss Gruffydd, the two women left, with many expressions of gratitude to Mr. Morrus for his generosity and good nature.

"Well, Nansi," said Mr. Morrus, turning to the old woman, "what is it that ails you this evening?"

"Empty cupboards, sir, as usual," said Nansi, "it's very hard on me sir, without a bite to eat for two days, at least nearly; and I've nobody to help me, you understand, a poor old lady like me, I don't know where to turn sir, and it being so cold sir, and me with no fire nor warmth of any sort in the house, let God be my witness, sir."

"Well, are you still drinking?" said Mr. Morrus.

"Drink!" said Nansi, "mercy, indeed I do not sir, not a drop for three years sir, or nearly, not a drop but clean water—that is, as clean as it comes in the house over there—one or two tadpoles or other little insects and the like. No, I drink nothing but water and a little tea, if I can get any; not that that's often, let God be my witness, sir."

"Indeed, the Lord God sees all, Nansi," said Mr. Morrus, "and I do hope you are telling me the truth."

"True as the lord's prayer sir, as God is my witness, sir" said Nansi.

"Very good. But truly, I haven't the time to speak to you this evening, Nansi; here you go, there's sixpence for you."

"Thank you, sir," said Nansi; "I hope you shan't miss it, sir, that's all I'll say. Though truly sir, it's a shame I'm not a pagan sir, living on the other side of the world, instead of a poor old Welsh woman living in the town like this, where everyone knows me and knows I'm an honest woman."

"Well, now what makes you say that, Nansi?" said Mr. Morrus.

"Oh!" said Nansi, "Why, if I were a pagan, sir, then ten pounds you'd give me, sir, not sixpence, and nice young women and ugly old ones would be rushing about to collect donations for me, sir, on cold, stormy nights— there'd be no need for me to wander about myself, sure there wouldn't sir! Oh, it is a shame I'm no pagan, and my face dark as a crow's sir, and living far, far from here!"

"Now, now, Nansi," said Morrus, seizing his chance when Nansi had stopped for breath, "Shouldn't you be grateful that you have the good fortune to live in a Christian country?"

"Indeed I have sir, sixpence worth of good fortune, sir!" said Nansi.

"Instead of those benighted lands," added Mr. Morrus, who had not listened to Nansi's response, "where they know nothing of God's word. No indeed, for shame, Nansi, you should be thankful—"

"For sixpence, sir? Well, but I have thanked you, sir. Man alive! How many times should you say I should thank you for sixpence, sir? Once each, I suppose, will that do? Now then, thank you, thank you, thank you, there that's three for you; thank you, thank you, thank you; and that's the six thank-yous for the sixpence, sir. Oh! I'm a lucky woman after, all sir, not to be a pagan sir; for when would I ever be finished giving thanks for ten pounds?!"

"Now, now, Nansi! If you do not think I have been generous enough with you, then I shall have to—"

"Oh, no, sir!" said Nansi, "surely you don't think I've yet to be thankful enough for the sixpence, sir, or are you wanting another six thank-yous for the sixpence, sir?"

"Off with you! Now—I've no more time to waste with you!"

"Good night, sir," said Nansi, "I hope you won't miss the sixpence sir—are you sure you're not doing yourself harm, sir, in giving it me? If so then perhaps it'd be better for me not to take it. Good night, sir!"

And out Nansi went, leaving Mr. Morrus to his exasperation.

"Well, I never saw the like!" he said aloud. "There's no pleasing her, ever, and the way she was envying even those poor pagans—why, there are some hard-nosed people in this world!"

Having thus voiced his thoughts, Mr. Morrus's mood improved somewhat, and having finished his accounts, he put on his overcoat, and set off out. It was, truthfully, a stormy and freezing cold night—March had come in as fierce as a lion—and there were few others out on the streets, especially those little streets where the quarry workers lived, and through which Mr. Morrus made his way home. There was one street whose houses had not been completely finished, though they were poor and lowly like others; and it was down this street that Mr. Morrus turned to make his way home.

Before he had gone ten yards he saw a man leaning against a wall. Naturally enough, Mr. Morrus assumed that he was a drunkard, and would not have paid the man any more attention had he not needed to pass alongside him, for he stood in his way on the pavement, and to have avoided him would have meant moving to the middle of the road which was filthy and uneven. So Mr. Morrus stayed his course, rather than giving the man a wide berth. As he approached the man moved aside to make room for him to pass, and Mr. Morrus thought he heard the sound of whimpering. That made him look at the man more closely, and he soon recognised him as one of his own workers.

"Hello, Joseff!" said Mr. Morrus, "What's the matter? What are you doing there on such a freezing cold night? Why don't you go home to be by the fire? I thought that you weren't well?"

"Well, I'm not well, no," said Joseff.

"Well then, what are you loitering here for? Have you been drinking?"

"Drinking!" said Joseff, "I never tasted so much as a drop of alcohol in my life, and regardless, even had I wanted some, I couldn't afford it."

"Well then, why don't you go home to the fireside then?"

"There is no fire," said Joseff, reluctantly. "The fact is, there's not a scrap of food or coal in the house."

"Well, well, what happened to your wage? Surely you can't have spent it already, you've only just received it yesterday—a month's wage!"

"It's gone, sir, every penny, to pay for food. Two pounds and ten shillings a month isn't much for a family of five to live on. Whatever I earn goes, goes, like water through a sieve!"

"Oh; well," said Mr. Morrus, "you must be careful not to run up debts, Joseff. I'm sure there's something you could have done, surely there must have been? Why weren't you more careful? Now, I know some months are harder than others, I know that. You must put money aside for the difficult months. Here, here's a half crown. Take it straight back home, and get yourself some food and warmth."

"Thank you, sir," said Joseff, and Mr. Morrus hurried on his way. Joseff stood on the path, the half crown in his hand, and thought about his situation. Having worked hard for a month in the quarry, he had earned two pounds and ten shillings, and every penny of those had gone, and it had not been half enough. His wife and his young family would suffer. His wife—yes, he could remember a time when there hadn't been a girl in the town who blushed as prettily as Elin, but where was that healthy blush now? And the little ones, what had they done, the poor innocents, to deserve this? And what was it he had done, and if it had been him, why should they suffer for it? Joseff broke down in tears, and wailed, "Oh, it can't be that this is right!"

"Joseff! What on earth are you doing out here in the cold?" said someone.

Joseff recognised the voice, and answered.

"Gwilym, my friend," he said, "it's all over for me."

"No it isn't, surely," said Gwilym, "Look; come with me, I'll take you home. We've just been discussing what to do, and next Saturday we'll put it to the men for a vote. It's just not reasonable to expect us to work under these terms, and not humane either. The most anyone earned in the quarry last week was four pounds."

"Yes, and if it comes to a strike, it will only get worse."

"I'm afraid of that too. But we have to do something. We can't go on like this. I'm just trying to keep the men from being rash."

"Hello, Joseff, you're out here, are you?" said Foul Mouthed Nansi, striding straight towards him, "Elin is out looking for you everywhere."

"What's the matter?" said Joseff, alarmed.

"Oh," said the old woman, "nothing in particular, I don't think, but she asked me to tell you to go home, if I saw you."

"Oh, thank you, Nansi, I shall," said Joseff. They had reached the end of the street where Joseff lived, Nansi following behind them. Suddenly someone came out of one of the houses a little way up the street, in floods of tears. It was a woman, and Gwilym, Joseff and Nansi went straight to meet her.

The woman saw them coming, and broke into a wail, "Oh, dear Gwen bach!"

Chapter VII.
The Death of Gwen Bach

Gwilym felt his heart sink on hearing the cry, and he knew immediately what had happened—his dear, affectionate little friend had passed beyond all suffering, for ever more.

"Oh, Joseff, Joseff, what will we do?" wailed Mrs. Tomos, "Gwen bach has—has—Oh, I can't say the word—she's gone!"

Joseff fell backwards, and would have fallen to the floor had Gwilym not caught him. "Gone!" he said. "Gone! Poverty, want, and death! Like hounds at our tails!"

"You have to hold yourself together," said Gwilym tenderly. "Try and hold yourself together, Joseff."

"And there he was telling me I shouldn't squander my wages!" said Joseff, as if to himself.

"Who was saying that?" asked Gwilym.

"Mr. Morrus. Oh, he's starved my dear little girl to death! And there's his half crown! I wish I could throw it in his face!"

"Half a crown!" said Nansi below her breath. "Good thing he didn't give me the last sixpence he had!"

"Half a crown!" said Gwilym fiercely. "If he paid his workers properly, his charity could go to hell!"

"Or better still, he could keep it for Nansi!" said the old woman.

"And tomorrow morning in chapel there he'll be, at the point of tears as he praises his own Christian spirit to the rest of that clutch of fools that people speak of as if they were saints!" said Gwilym. "Though I suppose a half crown of charity costs him less than five or six shillings more wages, however kind and generous it may look to give a half crown in charity. Oh, what injustice is done in the name of faith and charity!"

"Had you never understood that before now, young man?" said Nansi. "Just you wait until you're an old woman like me—"

"Well, now," said Gwilym, with a feeling that he had yielded too much control to his temper under the circumstances, "perhaps this isn't the place to speak of—"

"Yes, well, young man," said the determined Nansi, "let me tell you now, you'll be an old woman like me twice over before you see this world without more ill done in the name of faith and charity than anything else."

"Yes, well, but that's enough," said Gwilym, "don't talk so loudly."

"But it's true," said Nansi. "Why, Mr. Morrus gave me sixpence tonight, six pence, you know, six pennies! He gave half a crown to one of his own workers, and ten pounds to the pagans—"

"Pagans?" said one of the women nearby.

"Yes, pagans," said Nansi, as determined as ever, "black pagans. Collecting for the Mission or something, they were."

"The spell of foreign lands!" said Gwilym. "Charity begins at home!"

"Yes—with sixpence," said Nansi, "but it grows the further it goes—ten pounds!"

As this remarkable exchange was taking place they had all crowded around Joseff and his wife to comfort them; but Elin was soon wailing bitterly again, "Oh, dear Gwen!"

She was escorted into the house by some of the neighbours, and Gwilym and Joseff followed after them.

There, in a tiny cot beside the fireplace in the kitchen, lay the body of Gwen bach. Her face was very pale, but beautiful—Oh! so beautiful, her thick, yellow hair all about her like so many golden torcs. One of her hands lay beside her on the quilt, so tiny, so perfect, despite being so thin. One by one, as they saw the poor, dead child, the neighbours who had crowded in left in tears. Gwilym stayed by the bedside, staring at the tiny face. She lay there, divine in her beauty, so pure and innocent was she. Gwilym bent down and kissed the tiny face, which had already turned cold, before turning away with the others, his heart within him feeling as if it were sinking.

And what of the parents? They simply stood nearby, moving neither hand nor foot. Their little angel gone. The others turned away in their sadness; the father and mother stood in mute grief.

Old Nansi stood also, and in her turn, looked at the little girl.

"Oh!" she said, after some time, "I lost a little girl, three years old. Forty years ago that was, barely two months after poor Will was killed in the quarry. I can see her blond head and her little blue eyes this very minute. Oh, my dear little thing."

The old woman rushed from the house, but a few seconds later returned. "Don't break your heart, my girl," she said to Mrs. Tomos. "Forgive me, but I lost a little girl myself, forty years ago. Here, girl, take this loaf, have a bit to eat, or you'll get sick."

The old woman took a sixpenny loaf from her apron, put it on the table, and went to comfort the poor parents. Gwilym stole away, whispering to himself, *"Garwa'r golwg, gorau'r galon!"**

---

* *Garwa'r golwg, gorau'r galon.* "The rougher the look, the better the heart." This is an example of *cynghanedd*, the Welsh strict poetic metre: notice how the consonants repeat: g r r g l / g r r g l (w is a vowel in Welsh). Gwynn was a master of this kind of poetry, and loved to use or suggest *cynghanedd* in his prose too; the title of his second novel

Within a few days the day of Gwen bach's funeral had come. Instead of carrying her far, far to see the trees and the big mountains, and the sun, Gwilym carried her coffin to the graveyard. The big mountains were shrouded in thick fog, and yet, the sun shone through the cold murk of the mist onto the little freshly-dug grave. A great number of the quarrymen attended the funeral, standing in a circle about the grave, and sang the old hymn, *Bydd myrdd o ryfeddodau,*[*] and did so with that strength which only a choir of Welsh colliers or quarrymen can sing. Gwilym stood to one side, and once the people had gone their various ways he stayed behind with the gravedigger to finish attending to little Gwen's secluded resting place.

A stranger had been in the graveyard watching the funeral, and once the crowd departed the stranger made his way over towards Gwilym and the gravedigger. He was a man of some fifty years, perhaps older, his face showing clearly that his life had been one of no small degree of licentiousness, and furthermore one that had been spent in a country much hotter than Britain. The man came over towards the two men tidying the grave, and watched them for some time before asking,

"Who was it they were burying today?"

"The little daughter of one of the quarrymen," said Gwilym.

"Is that so?" said the stranger, and then went on to enquire about the church and its graveyard, seeming rather to want to draw out a conversation than anything else, for he seemed to barely listen to the gravedigger's answers, and directed almost every question at Gwilym.

Camwri Cwm Eryr, is a cynghanedd, and the alliterative *Gorchest Gwilym Bevan* hints at it.

[*] *Bydd Myrdd o Ryfeddodau.* 'There shall be a world of wonders.' The hymn was once popular at funerals.

For his part, Gwilym felt little desire to answer him: there was something in the man's face that made him feel as if he would prefer his absence to his company. Nevertheless, the stranger continued to try to draw him out. It was only when they had finished attending to the grave, and that Gwilym got up to leave, that the stranger finally departed. Gwilym made his way to his lodgings, whilst the stranger made for Bryn y Craig, the home of Mr. Morrus.

For the stranger was, in fact, none other than the younger brother of Mr. Morrus, who had arrived two days earlier and was staying with his brother and his family, much to their discomfort—some of them, at least. Richard Morrus had been very much the prodigal son of the pair, and had been the cause of no small distress to his parents. Richard had trained as a doctor, but had squandered his time and talents, and had come into some difficulty, and found it necessary to leave the country at short notice. He had not, in fact, been heard from in many years; indeed, nothing had been heard from him for such a long time that it had been assumed, if not indeed hoped, that he was deceased; and yet suddenly he had turned up again, in a somewhat unfortunate state, and invited himself to stay at his brother's house. By all accounts he had no intention of leaving in any great hurry. There was, no doubt, an interesting story regarding the years Richard had spent abroad, and yet all he would tell of said story to his brother and his family was that he had wandered far and wide, feeding himself—he said nothing of drink, but there was no need—however he was able.

For all his profligacy, Richard had always been polite, almost to a fault, a fact which had always endeared him greatly to Mr. Morrus; but as for Olwen, she could barely stand the man, with his "feigned manners," as she put it.

As Mr. Richard Morrus crossed the lawn towards the house, Olwen came to meet him.

"Well, Miss Olwen," said Richard, "I've been amusing myself in the graveyard."

"Oh really?" asked Olwen, "a strange place for amusements, I would have thought?"

"Well, yes indeed, but that's not what I meant. You ladies are so awfully curt that we men need to be very careful about how we talk to you. But I went for a walk, and whilst passing the graveyard, I saw a funeral, and stayed to look. They were burying the little girl of one of the quarrymen here, that's what I heard."

"Oh, yes, the poor thing!" said Olwen, more to herself than to her uncle, "that's the one Gwilym was talking about."

Richard heard her, and asked,

"Gwilym? Who's Gwilym?"

"Oh, he works in the quarry. I was speaking with him the other day, and he was telling me that the little girl had died."

"I'm sure he was the one that was with the gravedigger just now, tidying the grave at the end," said Richard, "I think it's Gwilym that the gravedigger called him. And that boy's at the quarry, is he? He's a clever look about him."

"He does, and he is the way he looks as well—like many of us," said Olwen, making little effort to hide the contempt in her voice.

"Quite so," said Richard. "He's from around here then, is he?"

"No—at least, I don't think so," said Olwen, "though no doubt you'd get more of his story by asking him yourself."

Olwen went on her way, feeling herself blush, and knowing full well that she would say something she'd regret if she continued her conversation with her uncle. Why on earth was he asking about Gwilym?

As for Richard, he went inside, shaking his head, and thinking to himself, "why, I thought that was the one I saw her speaking with the other day."

Why it was that Mr. Richard smiled as he said this, only he could say; though he would often boast of his ability to read people's hearts in their faces. He went into the house, and struck up a conversation with Mrs. Morrus, telling her all about the funeral, and delighting her with the various melancholy details of the occasion.

Having escaped her uncle, Olwen made her way along the road, crossing the fields along a footpath that led towards the mountains. She looked behind her several times as she went, but there was nothing to be seen of her uncle, and he could not possibly be able to see her now from the house. Though she would never have admitted it, Olwen felt cross with herself for looking behind her. What difference did it make to anyone else where she went, and why should she care who saw her? It was her uncle's fault, she thought. What business had he in asking her about Gwilym? As she thought such thoughts, Olwen crossed a field or two and came to a stone stile in the shadow of a copse of trees at the far end of one of the fields. There she waited, and soon enough Gwilym appeared, and within a few seconds was by her side.

The two shook hands, and then stood in silence by the stile, looking down at the plain below them. It was some time before either of them spoke, just as if each was waiting for the other to say something.

Finally, Olwen broke the silence.

"Well," said she, "here we are; I've come all this way up here at your request; though I don't see why you couldn't have met me somewhere else."

"Thank you for coming to meet me," said Gwilym. "It's only that I'd noticed at least three or four people staring at us as if we had horns on our heads when we were speaking on the road the other day."

"I don't doubt that, but what difference should that make to me?"

"Well, none, but I wouldn't like to put you in an awkward place."

"Well, well, there's no turning you, is there? Look, I tried my best, but I'm afraid my attempt didn't do anyone much good. My father wouldn't hear any of it, and when I told him how hard it was on Joseff Thomas and his family, he only insisted that that was all down to a lack of foresight."

"Well, there's no helping that," said Gwilym grimly. "I'm sorry to have put you through so much trouble, but I had to; it was as if something was making me ask you."

"Not at all, you needn't mention it. I would love it if there was something I could do, but there's no helping it, no matter what I try. My father's in a foul mood. His brother, who has none too pleasant a manner, has come to stay; and somehow my father doesn't seem to be overly enjoying the honour."

"I wonder if it was him that I saw heading that way earlier, after the funeral?"

"Quite likely. He had been in the graveyard, and I would have guessed from what he said that he had spoken to you."

"There was a stranger who spoke to me."

"A man with a rather Bacchanalian look, was he?"

"Yes, he was, now you mention it."

"That's him. Mr. Richard Morrus, my uncle and full blood relative. He's my father's brother. I can't stand the man, with his affectation and his bombast. He's my uncle, but that can't be helped. And he was quite brazen in asking about who—about you."

"I thought he had taken a fancy to me. He tried to draw a conversation from me at the graveyard, but I must say,

I felt rather like you towards him—I had no great desire to speak to him."

"Gwilym?"

Olwen's voice was completely different, earnest, and tender.

"What is it?" asked Gwilym.

"If he tries to have a conversation with you again, don't speak with him."

"Why? What's the matter?"

"I don't know, but something makes me think that no good could come of it. I've no particular reason to think so. I'm being unfair on him, no doubt. Truly, I hope I am. But I just can't stand the man. Please, tell me you'll have nothing to do with him, will you, Gwilym?"

"It was a feeling exactly like that that came over me when I spoke to him. I'm not sure what harm he can do to me, but as you've asked me already not to have anything to do with him, well, then I won't, not if he begs me on his hands and knees to speak to me."

"Alright. There it is then. I've no desire to go home just now. I must get up into the mountains again."

"Oh, no, you mustn't," said Gwilym, "just in case—"

But Olwen had already set off, and despite himself, Gwilym followed after her.

Chapter VIII.
Who Killed Joseff?

The morning after laying Gwen bach to rest, Joseff returned to work at the quarry. He wore the look of a broken man, as his colleagues said to one another when they saw his pale face and bruised body. Although they all laboured under the same difficult terms, few of the other quarrymen had suffered as much as Joseff had done. He was a shy, reserved man, fond of reading and of thinking. He had not ever complained, for charity would put a bigger dent in his conscience than in his hunger. He had chosen to suffer in silence, rather than beg from others. Both he and his wife suffered, for all they had went to their young children. It is not always the weakest who suffer the most. There were a number of poor unfortunates in Treganol who got by on half enough food and clothing, depending entirely on charity for both; but they did not suffer as Joseff had done. To beg did not pain them, but it was a blow to Joseff's very soul to receive that for which they were grateful.

As I have said, the morning after the funeral of Gwen bach, Joseff went to the quarry. In truth, he was in no fit state to leave the house. To do so was, in itself, a form of suicide. Had he tried to end his life through cutting his throat or hanging himself, the law would pounce, full of concern for his life, and he would soon be answering for himself before a host of corpulent judges. But as he was killing himself through working when not able, the law would not intervene, nor express the slightest concern for him. A thousand hearts might break, and the law not break her fast. Let one neck be broken, and bright with the glory of justice she shall rise!

Joseff's breakfast that morning had been a dry crust and a sip of water. The wealthy of this our nineteenth century will find that hard enough to believe. The worker knows better, and the more honest the worker, the more often he has to make do with bread and water. If there is a man who doubts that in these humane and Christian days there are those who must break their fast with bread and water, then let him live for a month on two pounds ten shillings, and he will find it easier to doubt that man who speaks of *Gwlad y Breintiau Mawrion* than doubt anyone who should happen to mention that honest men live on bread and water—and too little of that.[*]

Joseff climbed the rock with his partners, and set to their work, but Joseff felt as if his head were full of water, rising and falling constantly, constantly. Then he thought of Gwen bach, and then of his wife. His heart felt heavy, heavy, and was sinking lower, and beating slower, and his head felt as if it were shattered into a thousand pieces. The great depths rushed below, and Joseff felt as if he were sinking, sinking, sinking. No doubt a dozen men who had never in their lives felt hunger would conclude that Joseff had lost his senses when he did what he did next, for he lifted his hands to his head, yelled, "Oh, Lord!" and jumped over the precipice.

He fell like a stone, and fled beyond the reach of his worries forever. That poor, wretched man.

Perhaps he had indeed lost his senses. Yet whom other than one who had suffered as he had, and come through

---

[*] *Gwlad y Breintiau Mawrion.* "The Land of Great Privileges." This was a common way to describe Victorian Britain in the Welsh press which captured the zeitgeist; almost a century later they might say that they had 'never had it so good.'

it alive, had the right to make such a judgement? Several score of the other quarrymen were witness to what happened, for they heard his yell and looked up to see.

"Joseff has killed himself!"

Those were the words on the lips of more than a few of those who saw it, "Joseff has killed himself!" But had he?

The quarrymen crowded around the body and stood in silence beside it. His head had struck a sharp rock, it was awful to behold. The men looked away, that they need not have to.

Gwilym pushed his way through the crowd and kneeled beside the body. All life had gone.

"This is the end of an honest man, under a man who calls himself religious, in a country that calls itself Christian!" said Gwilym.

"What? What's the matter here—what has—who?" said Mr. Morrus, who had arrived whilst Gwilym was talking.

"This must surely be the end of things as they are here, sir," said Gwilym. "Here is this man, lying in his blood, his poor wife a widow and little children orphaned."

"Did he fall?" asked Mr. Morrus, his voice sympathetic.

"No, sir," answered one of the men, "he jumped over the edge, sir—"

"Lord preserve us!" said Mr. Morrus, "The man must have been witless!"

"He was hungry!" said Gwilym.

"To do such a thing," Mr. Morrus added, "and condemn his own soul!"

"Condemn his own soul?" said Gwilym. "It's another soul that will be damned for his—if any is at all!"

"What do you mean?" said Mr. Morrus.

"I mean that it's you, sir, that must take responsibility for this."

"Me?" said Mr. Morrus in surprise, and it was genuine surprise.

"What on earth do you mean, man? Am I to be responsible for putting brains in my workers' heads as well as money in their pockets?"

"Thank God that you aren't," said Gwilym, his blood boiling despite himself. "If you were, nobody here would have enough to do so much as walk about, unless you gave them more brains than you give them wages—"

"I say! Hold your tongue, man!" said Mr. Morrus fiercely. "Who put you in such a place to tell me how I should treat my workers?"

"The same one who taught me to say, 'Our Father, which art in heaven,'" said Gwilym.

"Now hear this!" said Mr. Morrus in agitation. "Don't you start making a mockery of religion and its sacred things in my hearing—"

"Forgive me," said Gwilym, "if I let my temper get the better of me, but I am not mocking religion, and excuse me for saying that what you're saying now looks very much like boasting your religion over the dead body of the man your religion let die like this!"

There was a murmur of agreement from the assembled men, but Mr. Morrus cried loudly, half wailed in fact, "Silence! And you—understand that your service will no longer be required here a week from Saturday!"

"Very well, sir," said Gwilym quietly.

Joseff's body was carried down to a room alongside the office, and the doctor would arrive shortly afterwards, though too late, of course.

The office was quite a bit lower down than the quarry, and the road ran past it. The story of the tragedy spread like wildfire, and women rushed in their droves to the doorways of the houses on the lower side of the road to listen and see what had happened. Just as the men were carrying their fellow worker's body into the room, one of the Post Office boys came in with a telegram for Mr. Morrus, who took it into his study to read it. He opened it, and read it, and despite the serious and tragic event that had just taken place Mr. Morrus could not suppress the smile that appeared on his face. Arthur, his son, had succeeded in his attempt to secure a significant order from a large company on the Continent.

Now, Mr. Morrus was not an unfeeling man; indeed, there was a great deal of kindness in his nature, but when a man learns of his own son's success it is difficult for him to think any more of anyone else's son, even when he is lying dead in the next room. Furthermore, Arthur Morrus had shown such a lack of interest in commerce, and indeed in anything except study, and yet here was proof that he had changed. Mr. Morrus thought of the money that he had spent on his son's education, and of his own worries and prayers on his behalf, and it gave him great pleasure to think that Arthur had finally started to "take hold of things". Privately, he thought of how he would soon be too old to look after the business, and that he could now consider handing it over to the boy, and of spending the rest of his life in quiet contentment and rest. If, indeed, if the mine at Llan-y-Coed should also turn out successful, well, now then the boy would be on his feet!

These thoughts swept all others from Mr. Morrus's head, as they would have for nine men out of ten no doubt, but he was summoned back from his castles in the air by a man singing in the street below. The broken, dolorous voice sang:

> *"Disgwyl pethau gwych i ddyfod,*
> *Croesi hynny maent yn dod;*
> *Meddwl fory daw gorfoledd,*
> *Fory'r tristwch mwya 'rioed."*

(Waiting for wondrous things to come,
Crossing, here they come;
Thinking tomorrow shall come glory,
After the greatest sadness ever known.)

"Sadness!" said Mr. Morrus to himself, "strange that that creature should sing that verse just now. But that's just how life is, after all. Whilst I celebrate, there's Joseff's family in mourning. Thanks be for all mercies!"

Mr. Morrus set off to inform his wife of Arthur's success, and the voice in the street sang still,

*"Meddwl fory daw gorfoledd,
Fory'r tristwch mwya 'rioed."*

"Sadness!" said Gwilym, standing beside his friend's dead body. "Sing on, whoever you are, never was that verse sung on so appropriate an occasion! But pity the poor man: he cannot even lighten his burden by thinking that there may come glory tomorrow, for the sadness today is too much!"

There's little need to tell what happened next. Twelve good men were brought together—tradesmen, and men who lived on their own wealth—and an inquest was carried out on Joseff's body. Evidence was given by a few of the other quarry workers, along with the evidence from the doctor and the policemen, and it was determined that Joseff had committed suicide by leaping from the cliffside, having lost his wits. And that was it—apart from an expression of sympathy for the widow and orphans, as the *Flame* reported on the following Saturday.

Joseff was laid to rest in the earth alongside his little daughter less than three days after she herself had been placed there. Every last one of the quarry workers attended the funeral, and having laid six feet of earth on

Joseff's coffin and sung "*Bydd Myrdd o Ryfeddodau*", the crowd slowly dispersed.

But the workers were restless, and one by one, they made their way to the Old Quarry. Not a word had been spoken about any meeting, but somehow they all felt drawn together. Less than half an hour after the funeral every worker in Chwarel y Coed had assembled in the Old Quarry, and the meeting began, as it usually did, with the hymn "*O, Arglwydd Dduw Rhagluniaeth.*" Gwilym was there, and once the singing was finished he was called upon to speak, which he did.

Gwilym was a natural and enthusiastic public speaker, but this time he avoided saying anything to excite his colleagues, and when he had finished there were whispers that Gwilym had not spoken as well as he usually did; and some attributed this to a lack of investment in the cause now that Mr. Morrus had given him notice that he would no longer be employed at the quarry. There were other speakers, some fervent ones, and the men became quite agitated. Those speakers were good men, and they had not intended to do anything overly impulsive or unwise, and yet there was little of the stuff of a real leader in any of them. They said things which were, without a doubt, true, and yet they were things which tended to make the listener hot-headed. The only one present who was truly worthy to lead the others now felt that he had no right to say anything at all, as his employment was to be terminated, and he no longer had a personal stake in the men's fight.

Gwilym told them as much when he was pressured into speaking once again, but the workers quickly showed how easily they could misunderstand, as he was promptly asked whether he was abandoning them. There was no choice left to him then, of course, other than to put himself at their service, and so he told them that he was ready to do so. This was met with loud cheers of approval, and a number of them lifted Gwilym up on their shoulders and went on to parade through the streets, singing as they went, their hero held above them as if they were showing him off.

As they turned up Stryd y Graig* to escort Gwilym to his lodgings, Gwilym noticed a man standing in the doorway of one of the taverns. It was Richard Morrus, Mr. Morrus's brother, standing to watch the procession. His face bore a smile of sorts, and once again Gwilym felt as he had when he had first seen the man in the graveyard the day of Gwen bach's funeral: a kind of instinctive revulsion toward the man.

But the men carried him onwards, singing still, and Richard Morrus smiled again, wider this time, and whispered to himself, "Well, it looks like my dear brother is in for some trouble. Ah, there's the leader—the man who was out with Miss Olwen Morrus across the fields the other day!"

Richard Morrus made for Bryn y Graig, and soon found Olwen, alone. "Miss Olwen," said he, "do you remember me making the observation to you the other day that that young man—what was his name, Gwilym, was it?—that he had a clever look about him?"

"I do," said Olwen. "Why, what's happened? Have you changed your mind?"

"Not at all," said Richard, "but it looks like he's the leader of the quarry workers here. They had him up on their shoulders, parading through the town just now."

"Well, do you suppose that that was because of the clever look he has?" said Olwen.

"No," said Richard, refusing to rise to the bait, "I was thinking that at some point he must have been associating

---

* *Stryd y Graig.* Literally 'Rock Street' but in that context more likely to refer to a crag or cliff.

with cultured and sophisticated people, even if he doesn't now."

"It's quite possible," said Olwen sternly, "after all, I don't think he ever went to university."

"Ha! So you know his story, then?"

"No, I don't, but you can tell from the colour of his nose that he hasn't learned those things that some learn at university."

This was too much for Richard, niceties or not, and he swore, quite coarsely.

"Now you look here, Miss," he said. "You're best not going down that path with me. I know more than you think. I know who was standing with Gwilym Bevan up by the gate on Lôn y Fron* the other night, and who was striding out over the fields with him to the mountains a few days ago."

"So do I," said Olwen, "and if watching what other people do brings you any pleasure, then by all means, watch away, of course. It doesn't make any difference to me. I enjoy the company of those who have some understanding about them: I can't stand those creatures who've attained that level of development where the animal has learned to talk, but not yet learned to think. On which note, good day to you, Mr. Richard Morrus!"

Olwen departed, leaving her uncle not quite sure what to do: whether he should go straight to her father, or wait and see what happened next.

---

* *Lôn y Fron*. Bron or Fron can mean various things but in this context it means a hillside or slope, so this might be 'hill lane'.

Chapter IX.
The Strike

The floodgates were opening. The workers had decided that they would strike unless improved terms were offered, and they had appointed Gwilym and three others to present an ultimatum to that effect to Mr. Morrus. He in turn had reluctantly agreed to receive the deputation, and there he was one evening, in his quarry-side office, awaiting the appointed time when the deputation would arrive. They did so.

"Well," said Mr. Morrus, sitting himself comfortably in his chair, the men standing before him.

"Well," he said again, "here you are then. I would appreciate it if you could say what you have to say, and do so promptly, for I've little time to waste, you know."

"Please excuse me, sir," said Gwilym, "but my colleagues have asked me to speak to you on their behalf. I urged them to appoint someone else, as, for a number of reasons I did not consider myself an appropriate spokesperson; nevertheless my advice was rejected, and thus I am acting in accordance with their wishes. In doing so, of course, I need not remind you to leave me out of all considerations, as I will, as you know, be leaving your employment. I'm confident, therefore, that you will not allow your personal feelings towards myself to affect your treatment of the men—"

"That's enough," said Mr. Morrus, impatiently, "and I would appreciate it if you did not presume to decide what my personal feelings are towards you or anyone else. Could we keep this brief? What do you have to say?"

"Very well," said Gwilym, "we have come here on behalf of the men, all of them, to ask you for improved terms under which to work."

"Is that so," answered Mr. Morrus dryly, "then I'm afraid to say that I am not in a position to grant your request. If the terms are not to your satisfaction, then there is nothing to prevent you seeking better terms elsewhere."

"In that case, sir, then you are forcing our hand."

Mr. Morrus had not expected this. For one moment he did not know what to do, but he soon composed himself and decided that the best course of action would be to hold his ground, for he was convinced that there was no danger the men would defeat him.

"What?" said Mr. Morrus, "are you men—"

Before he could finish the sentence the office door burst open, and someone rushed in yelling, "The lead! The lead! The lead, sir! Here it is, Captain Parri sent me to show it you—"

The man with the lead ore began to prance about on the spot, rather unsteadily. Mr. Morrus turned to him and said,

"Quiet a minute, Siôn, quiet. I'll speak to you presently."

And then Mr. Morrus turned to the rest and asked them, "Are you, men, going to let your heads be turned—"

"Forgive me, sir," said Gwilym, "but—"

"That's it, lad," said Siôn, attempting to steady himself, "that's it, tell him to take a look at the lead—"

"Will you be quiet, man!" said Mr. Morrus, at which Siôn calmed down a little.

"Do you, you men, who've worked this quarry your whole lives, wish to be led astray like this by some strange foreign—"

"Forgive me, sir," said Gwilym, "but in truth, I'm leading no-one. The only reason I'm here talking at all is that the men themselves insisted, I suppose because I find speaking easier than many of them do. I'm doing nothing but setting out their case before you, sir, and with that in mind, I hope you will have no objections, and that you will speak to me, in accordance with your own views, sir."

"And to me too, sir," said Siôn. "There's not a man on the earth who ever saw a better vein of lead, no, by—"

"Be quiet, Siôn," said Mr. Morrus. "And as for you," he said, turning to face Gwilym, "I refuse to acknowledge you; and what, pray tell, is your meaning in asking me to act in accordance with my own views?"

"Lead, sir, that's my meaning," Siôn interrupted. "I never saw a man with a better idea for good lead ore, sir, and here you are, you won't even look at it!"

"For goodness' sake, Siôn, do be quiet, or you shall have to leave," said Mr. Morrus. "Explain your meaning, young man," he said, turning back to look at Gwilym.

"Well, sir," said Gwilym, "I hadn't intended to bring it up, but as I happened to mention it, I shall answer your question. Some time ago I heard you speaking, sir, on a public platform, about justice for the workers—"

"I see," said Mr. Morrus.

"See it, sir? Why of course, man," said Siôn, reaching into his pocket for something, but Gwilym pressed on, and this time Mr. Morrus paid no attention to Siôn.

"I heard you," said Gwilym, "if you'll excuse my mentioning it, speaking of the importance of unity between workers, or at least, that was the effect of your words to my ears, sir, and I heard you preaching justice between men—"

"Silence!" said Mr. Morrus, "I shall be the judge of what I did or didn't say."

"Indeed, quite so," said Gwilym. "I don't deny you that right, sir, and I'm sure you will, in the same way, permit us to decide what we have to say."

"If the terms under which you work are not to your satisfaction," said Mr. Morrus, agitated, "well, there's no helping that. I cannot offer you any better."

"In that case," said Gwilym calmly, "then we shall strike."

"It was Capten Parri that struck the vein, what's he talking about?" said Siôn, but Mr. Morrus was not paying him the slightest bit of attention now. He stood up, and, turning to Gwilym and his comrades, said to them,

"If you men choose to be led astray by strangers with wild ideas, like this one, then there's no helping you. Follow your course. Strike, if that's what you want. You have my answer—you can work under the same terms, or you can strike."

"Very well sir, then we shall strike," said Gwilym, and he and his three comrades left the office, leaving Mr. Morrus and Siôn.

"Now, sir," said Siôn, "the captain's sent me with some of the lead for you to see."

"Well, now," said Mr. Morrus, "what on earth is the matter with you, Siôn?"

"Oh, only the lead, sir," answered Siôn, "here it is, we've just struck it, we have, and I was so happy sir, as you can see, that I may have been a bit excessive with the celebrations, to tell you the truth, now, the truth that is. But here's a piece of the lead, sir, and there's plenty of it, plenty. The captain danced when we struck the vein, sir, he danced like this."

Siôn began to dance, but either he lacked the skill or else he was too light-headed, for he immediately fell flat on the floor, and started rolling about.

"Well, well," said Mr. Morrus. "It pains me to see you drunk like this, Siôn. You must stop this at once, and promise me you'll take the pledge."

"I shall, sir," said Siôn, who had climbed unsteadily to his feet again, "but the captain wants to see you, sir. When will you come down?"

Somehow, though he was standing still, Siôn tripped, and fell flat on the floor once again.

"I hope," he said, "that you don't come down like that, sir—it goes to my legs, sir, you see. Oh! The lead, that's where the lead is—not in my legs, I mean, either, but in the mine, sir. That's where the lead is, the mine!"

"Well," said Mr. Morrus, "tell the captain I shall come down tomorrow, or the next day at the latest, Siôn, and you go straight home, now."

"As straight as I can, sir," said Siôn.

"And you mind I don't hear that you've been stalking those pubs again."

"Alright sir, I'll take as much care as I can that you never hear any such thing, sir. Good night, sir, good night."

And Siôn left, whispering to himself, "There you are, captain! That'll keep the mine going a while yet!" Siôn staggered onwards until he had reached the edge of town. Then, all signs of intoxication suddenly disappeared, and he started striding briskly and surely in the direction of Captain Parri's home. He arrived at last and went straight in, and there was the captain waiting for him, and another man. This was none other than our associate, Mr. Richard Morrus.

"Well," said the Captain, "did you see him, Siôn?"

"I did, Captain," said Siôn, "I think that lead has settled him. I pretended to him that I was under the influence, I did, so as to keep him from asking too many questions. He said he'd come down tomorrow or the day after at the latest."

"There we are, that'll do nicely," said the Captain.

"It will," said Richard, "for all that he's so cunning when it comes to everything else, he's blind enough when it comes to mining."

"It sounds like there's going to be trouble in the quarry," said Siôn. "When I was there today there were four men speaking to him on behalf of the workers, and telling him they were going to go on strike."

"Ha! Is that so?" said Richard, "and was one of the men a young man, maybe twenty-five, a handsome young man with fair hair?"

"He was," said Siôn. "He was the main speaker, and he was really getting under Mister's skin too."

"Is that so! That's what I thought!" said Richard Morrus.

"What is?" asked Captain Parri.

"Oh," answered Richard, "I was thinking that that was the man who was leading the workers, and him such good friends with the master's daughter!"

"Oh, it's like that, is it?" said Captain Parri. "It's going to get a bit lively then, no?"

"It is," said Richard, "and I'd like to stay and see it, but I shall need to go away for a while now."

The three stayed to smoke and drink for an hour or two. Richard Morrus and Captain Parri were old friends, and had spent many an hour drinking together when they were younger. To a large degree, they were both men who lived by their wits, though the Captain had stayed in his own country, and had succeeded in keeping his schemes from coming to light, so far. When Richard had returned he had found the Captain, and renewed their acquaintance. It was a natural enough thing for Richard to visit the lead mine in which his brother had invested so heavily, and of which his old friend was Captain; but Richard was not a man to visit a lead mine with his eyes closed. He saw at once that there was very little hope that the mine would ever turn a profit, and saw at once what the Captain was up to. As was previously noted, Richard had precious little means of his own, and saw a chance to take a cut of the profit his friend the Captain was making from the mine. He had therefore given notice to the Captain that he knew fairly well where things stood, and the long and the short of it was that he and the Captain had come to an understanding. Richard's only duty, under the terms of the agreement between him and his old friend, was to keep his mouth shut, an arrangement which suited Richard very well.

The two friends spent most of the night speaking of the good old days, drinking and smoking, and the following morning Richard Morrus departed, though let his friend know that he would return soon. Richard had already informed the family at Bryn y Graig that he would be going on a trip, and Mr. Morrus and Olwen, if not perhaps Mrs. Morrus, were very pleased to hear it; particularly because Arthur was expected home soon.

Arthur Morrus, as I mentioned earlier, had spent some years in one of the English Universities. He had earned his degree, and had then spent some time travelling the Continent, a trip which his father had ensured would include a number of business opportunities on his behalf. Mr. Morrus had at one point hoped that Arthur would take up preaching, and for this reason he had given him the best education he could; though it had quickly become apparent that his son had little chance of becoming a minister. This had been a source of considerable disappointment to Mr. Morrus, and yet he had permitted Arthur to finish his course at University and earn his degree, and then sanctioned his travels abroad as well, on the agreement that he would then join his father in the business. Arthur had travelled widely and had, more by accident than anything else, succeeded in signing a deal with a German trading company on his father's behalf.* It was news of this deal which had brought Mr. Morrus such joy on the day of Joseff's death, and he was now impatient to see Arthur return home so that he would be able to immerse himself in the world of business, and in doing so forget some of those strange ideas which Mr. Morrus had reason to believe his son might be harbouring.

Work stopped at Craig y Coed quarry, and a sepulchral silence fell upon Treganol. Mr. Morrus had not once thought that the men really would refuse to work, and so when they did so, he felt incensed that they had dared to defy him so. He would have no talk of yielding to their demands, and would not even entertain it privately, and so it was: day after day, the silence in Treganol grew deeper. Crowds of workers were seen gathered on street corners to discuss things, and as the strike wore on some of the men found work elsewhere; though there was little to be had anywhere, and the majority of the workers simply stayed idle at home, waging their battle through suffering in silence, and through watching helplessly as their wives and children suffered also. Some relief was sent from other quarries nearby, and from some of the workers' unions in England, but the sum total received was not half enough to meet the needs of the workers and their families. As the days wore on the town became quieter and quieter. People even talked quietly, their deep voices turned furtive whispers. Rarely was the sound of laughter heard in the streets, and very soon the little children ceased their playing and running; they went to school, but did so quietly, and gloomily. It was clear that something was deeply wrong in Treganol. Some blamed the master, others his workers, and there was no shortage

---

* Slate from Welsh quarries was, and to some extent still is, used to roof houses all over Europe.

of that class of people who believe that half a loaf, however gained, is better than no loaf at all. Nevertheless, the town supported the workers' fund with no small amount in donations, whether gladly or reluctantly, and all that was received was carefully shared between the workers and their families.

One afternoon Arthur Morrus came home, though he had not been expected for another week. He walked from the station into the street, and immediately noticed the lifelessness that hung about the place, and in the people's faces. What was the matter? He met a young man in the street: he wore a sad, gloomy expression on his face, and yet that face was earnest and intelligent all the same.

"Can you tell me why this place is so quiet and lifeless?" asked Arthur Morrus.

"There's a strike at the quarry," said the young man.

"So I see; I'm sorry to hear that," said Arthur Morrus. "What caused the strike?"

Gwilym (for it was he) told Arthur all about the dispute and the strike, and Arthur Morrus listened attentively.

"Are you a member of the strike committee?" asked Arthur.

"Yes," was Gwilym's answer.

"Well then; here, have a few shillings for the fund. We'll see if there's something we can do. Good afternoon to you."

Arthur Morrus set off, and Gwilym stood for some time watching him go, whispering to himself: "His voice was just like hers!"

Chapter X.
The Rights of Man

Arthur felt restless and uneasy, and found it hard to make small talk with his parents, particularly his father, as the state of things in Treganol had made the young man pensive and uncommunicative. His mother assumed he was ill, and his father attributed it to a general disappointment and lack of enthusiasm for the world of business that was opening up in front of him. Olwen knew, however, that something besides these was the cause of his gloom, and soon found out the cause. The two spoke together at some length, and then both went out, leaving Mr. Morrus and Mrs. Morrus in the library.

The two sat facing each other, and Mr. Morrus knew that something was on his wife's mind, for she was continuously pleating and un-pleating her apron. This tic was Mrs. Morrus's general introduction to the raising of any subject, whatever it might be.

The pleating and un-pleating went on for some time, with a greater than usual intensity and attention to detail, and Mr. Morrus began to wonder what on earth the matter could be.

"Tomos," said Mrs. Morrus at length.

"Yes, my love," said Mr. Morrus, whom, it cannot be denied, was one of the best husbands. "What's the matter, my love?"

"I'm afraid," said Mrs. Morrus in a worried voice, "I'm afraid, Tomos dear, I'm afraid—"

"Well, afraid of what, my love?" said Mr. Morrus.

"I'm afraid, afraid that the boy's gotten some strange, wild ideas in his head, Tomos dear. He was discussing all sorts of strange things with Olwen just now."

"What was he discussing, my love?"

"The strike, Tomos, and he was saying that the men shouldn't have to strike, that every man has a right to live in this world without asking permission from anyone, and that God can't have made men just to starve them."

"Oh, I imagine he was talking in general terms, Hannah; I'm sure he would never dare think that I am to blame for the men's stubbornness."

"Oh! I really don't know," said Mrs. Morrus, more worried than before. "He was talking about someone, I don't know who, someone with an important sounding name, Skillus, or something like that, and apparently he spoke about the Prince of Immortals having his fun with some wretches.[*] I'm ever so worried that he's gone and picked up some wild ideas from somewhere! I was worried when he went to that university to be among all those Englishmen and foreigners that he'd turn into some obstinate—"

"Oh, don't you worry, my love," said Mr. Morrus heartily, "I'm sure the boy just didn't understand the situation, and that he wasn't talking about things as they are here right now. Young men are always thinking a great deal about things that look like complete nonsense to their elders, but time, and the weight of years, bring things together, every time."

Just as Mr. Morrus finished expressing this, Arthur came in and sat next to his mother.

"What's going on at the quarry, father?" he asked. "I hear the men are on strike—that's one of the first things

---

[*] This is possibly meant to be Schiller, but it is hard to tell, as Mrs. Morrus is supposed to be mishearing it.

I heard when I got home, and I was very sorry to hear it too.”

“Yes, they’ve let themselves be talked into striking,” said Mr. Morrus. “Don’t ask me about that right now, Arthur bach—I’m going to the school meeting in Bryn Glas Chapel, and need to think of something to say there.”
*

“Well, really,” said Arthur, “I wouldn’t be able to think of anything to say either, let alone say it, with several hundred of my fellow-men out of work, and with the weather like this.”

“What do you mean?” said Mr. Morrus. “It’s their fault, my boy. I didn’t turn them away, they left work of their own free will, and if they prefer starvation to working under the agreed terms, well, then I can hardly be blamed.”

“How much do they earn?”

“Well, that depends how hard they work.”

“From what I understand, the wages are very small, and the hours very long. You can’t deny that, father.”

“Well, I could find plenty of men who’d be glad of the work, if I looked for them.”

“No doubt you could, but why, do you think? Not because of the wages, but because the workers’ standard of living is too low. There’s no pride in such work, and living under such conditions demeans men, rather than elevates them.”

“Yes, yes,” said Mr. Morrus, “it’s all very well for you, you with your theories and your principles, to find fault with things, my boy, but just you try and change them and you’ll soon see that you have to accept things as they are. Talking is easy, but action always very difficult. With society as it is, it would be futile for one man to try and

---

* *Bryn Glas Chapel.* Green Hill Chapel. ‘School’ in this sense refers to what we might now refer to as a bible study class.

go against it; and if I tried it would be curtains for me soon enough."

"Yes," said Arthur, who was only warming up, "but you know full well, father, that that's just dodging the question. Just as you say, talking's easy, action difficult. I'm of the same opinion as yourself, if you let me say it. You yourself have spoken many times about the need for unity and an eight-hour working day—at the very least you have supported men who were in favour of those things—but now you say that action is difficult. And quite apart from that, I cannot forget the fact that you are a Christian, and if Jesus Christ was trying to do anything at all, then he was trying to improve the lot of the poor—"

"Oh, my dear boy!" cried Mrs. Morrus, who had been listening quietly so far. "Oh, my boy, you mustn't speak like that to your dear father, who raised you so well—now, you know he's sure to be right, Arthur bach!"

"I don't know about that, mother," said Arthur. "Nobody is infallible, and I cannot for the life of me see how my father's behaviour is consistent with—"

"Oh, Arthur, Arthur!" cried Mrs. Morrus in shock.

"So, that's how you come home, is it?" said Mr. Morrus, turning fierce. "That's what your university did to you, did it? Have you read and believed those faithless English wastrels who reduce the Saviour to nothing more than the leader of a pack of disgruntled layabouts? If you reduced their hours they'll only spend the time in the pubs, and it's far better that they spend their time at work than polluting themselves in such places. And you've learned to admire those worms who teach such things better than your own father, have you?"

"Don't cry," said Arthur, kissing his mother tenderly. "It's not a question of admiration, father, but of justice and fairness. It pains me to contradict you, but one doesn't have to go out of one's way to find bad things to say about those who profess to want to elevate and improve the masses, nor to insult the workers either: the truth is it's none of anyone else's business where they spend their time. If ten hours a day of dull, monotonous and uninteresting labour isn't worth more than these men here earn whilst doing it, then that surprises me very much; and what's more, you should remember that the quality of the rock makes a big difference. I understand that whilst there are similar terms in some other quarries, the rock is much easier to work. You should remember that some modern ideas are starting—"

"Stuff and nonsense!" said Mr. Morrus impatiently.

"Yes, well," said Arthur, "it's easy to say 'stuff and nonsense', but I remember you teaching me that all men were brothers, and that Jesus Christ had died for us all. I can also see, and it pains me to do so, that it's easy to believe such things without putting them into practice."

"Oh, my dear boy!" said Mrs. Morrus, "surely you aren't denying your Saviour? Oh, Arthur, Arthur!"

"Ah yes," said Mr. Morrus, his face red with rage, "and those are the modern ideas you're talking about, are they? Is that what you believe, after years of education, which cost me dearly? Why, if I'd known that, I'd have put you to work in the quarry! And you come home to break your mother and your father's hearts, with your atheistic and half-baked ideas? After my long hours of labour on your behalf, and after I've made ready to turn everything over to you, you've come home from university and now you are speaking against me, speaking scornfully of the faith of your fathers, and accusing your own father of doing injustice unto others. We'll have none of your irreligious ideas here, no thank you!"

"Father," said Arthur, "forgive me for speaking further. God himself knows that I do not want to cause you any pain, but I would rather die without a penny to my name than think that what I owned had been earned through ruining the lives of my fellow man! I can't help it, it's the truth. And remember, father, that I never said a word about atheistic ideas; it was you that brought them up. But if believing that a man shouldn't starve because he won't work for too small a wage is an atheistic idea, well then, call me an atheist if you like, and I shall be proud to call myself one. The education you provided has shown that much to me, at least, and I can't do anything about that."

Arthur left the room. Mrs. Morrus folded her arms and exclaimed in fright, "Oh, Arthur, Arthur, what shall become of the boy?"

"Yes," said Mr. Morrus, "oh, Lord, has it come to this after all, all the care and prayer, the worry and the encouragement and the expense? Oh, why has this happened?"

As this argument was going on at Bryn y Graig, Gwilym was sitting in his bare room, reading and thinking, and occasionally speaking his mind out loud, though there was nobody there to hear him. By now he had very few books left, for he had sold a great number of them for money to buy food. Placed on the tiny table before him were three or four books, and Gwilym eyed them mournfully. One of them was open, and Gwilym read a sentence or two out loud every now and then, before considering its content and meaning. Presently, he read, *Bags and crags have the same result on rags.* "Yes," he said to himself, "that's the gospel according to Ruskin, and there's more than just poetic elegance to the words—they hold a bitter truth. The fact is that the Bag-barons set themselves up as the leaders of freedom, and the people believe them!"[*]

---

[*] John Ruskin, *The Crown of Wild Olive*, 1866.

The young man was silent for a second, and then whispered again, "But what good is Ruskin, or anyone else, no matter how excellent, to a hungry man? They must go, and yet, it's hard to part with these dear old friends!"

He picked up the books and looked over them at length, turning the pages carefully, one after the other, and studying them intently. There was hardly a page there that he could not have recited almost from memory, and yet, they would have to go. Here and there the pages were marked with the print of a not-entirely-clean finger or thumb, and candle wax had been spilled on the occasional page. Gwilym could remember well the places he'd been where he'd read those books, and how those marks and stains had reached the pages. Even in London, at the height of his troubles, he had found joy in those books, and through every trial and difficulty so far he had managed to keep them, and yet, now they were the only things standing between himself and starvation, and they had to go. The best he could hope to receive for them was a few pennies at most, but what else could he do? Gwilym collected the books together once more and gave each one a second look, one after the other. Which one should go first? A difficult choice to make. Some of those books were the work of those who had suffered as he had; one of them was the work of a man who had died in the name of freedom: a man exiled from his own country, who had died, friendless, in a country on the altar of whose freedom he had sacrificed his own life; a man buried in anonymity; and denigrated by inconsequential men so utterly lacking in understanding and heart as to be unfit to tie his shoelaces.[*]

---

[*] My interpretation of this passage is that the man in question is Jesus, if we understand 'exile' to mean from heaven. Marx is another possibility, someone Gwynn would have been familiar with and someone whom it might have been controversial to name explicitly, but less likely to be familiar to the average reader.

Ah, what book should be first to go, and when it went, whichever one it was, how big the gap it would leave behind! It was easier to endure hunger than part with the books. Almost. How cruelly could man treat his fellow man, and how lifeless must men's consciences be. Would the day ever come when that conscience would awaken which would see the world made equal? "Every valley shall be exalted, and every mountain and hill shall be made low," the Bible said. Would that come to pass? "Bread shall be given him; his waters shall be sure." When would that time come? "In his days shall the righteous flourish," but when would those days come? Oh, such fine, valuable promises; but when would they all come to pass? And yet, the books had to go, for hunger was at the door.

"Gnaw, gnaw, gnaw, famine!" whispered the wretch, "yet it is easier to endure the bite of hunger than of conscience."

Someone knocked lightly at the door, and Gwilym rose to answer it. "It'll be one of the men again," he said to himself whilst crossing the room. "I'm almost afraid to see them!"

Gwilym opened the door, but it was not one of the men. Olwen slipped past him into the room.

Chapter XI.
Love and Duty

"Good morning, Miss Morrus," said Gwilym. "Please sit down, and please excuse what a gloomy place you'll find here. It's very hard on us, all of us, these days."

"Please, don't move to make space for me. I'm only calling by to look in on you, and it won't do for me to stay long. I prefer to stand next to you; there, that's it. I've been seeing some of the poor women, and I fear for them so, and the little children! Don't you think it would be better for the men to go back to work—the little children are suffering so!"

"They are," said Gwilym, "they are suffering, but the men are fighting for their rights, and I cannot call for them to return to work under the old terms, not until the bitter end, at least."

"But think of the suffering! I'm sure that if you told them to go, that the men would go, I know they would, and think of the suffering they all—"

"I don't need to think to know how they are suffering—I'm suffering in the same way, as they are. Your—your father has dismissed me—"

"Gwilym!"

"He has," said Gwilym, "and if the men returned to work tomorrow I should not go with them; and yet as I spoke on their behalf at the beginning, I will stand by them, to the end; and then, I shall go."

"Where will you go?"

"Well, I don't know, but I shall have to go, somewhere."

"Oh, Gwilym, don't go away!"

"Well, I won't go before the end, whatever end that may be. I shall suffer with the men, I can't abandon them now."

Olwen was silent. "Gwilym," she said presently, "please, don't go. I can't bear to think of, of—oh, just say you won't go! Here, take this, please, please don't refuse it, Gwilym."

Olwen took a purse from her pocket and placed it on the table, but Gwilym pushed it away.

"Miss Morrus," he said, "you and I were, and we still are, despite everything, we're—we're friends—and truly, I shall never forget my debt to you, and I'm grateful of course for your sympathy—"

Gwilym's voice was tender, and it took him a great effort to keep speaking dispassionately. Olwen looked down, and tears came to her eyes when she heard the word 'sympathy'; and yet she said nothing.

"But really," said Gwilym, "I'm sure your father wouldn't like to hear that you've come here to see me like this—"

"Oh, to see you? Why, I wonder?" said Olwen bitterly, but then stopped herself, and then added, pleadingly, "Look, Gwilym, take this. There's not much in it, but take it, from me."

"No," said Gwilym, "I can't take it, even from you— you must understand why."*

"Well," said Olwen, "yes, I know why. But I want to give you something—something to remember me by; I don't know why. Here, take my ring, and keep it, for my sake. I have a terrible fear that something is going to happen. Take this, to—to—"

Olwen burst into tears, and taking a ring from her finger, she offered it to Gwilym.

---

* All donations were to be shared equally between the strik-ers.

"Really, I can't," said Gwilym, "but thank you, thank you with all my heart, for your sympathy—"

"Oh, what good is sympathy!" said Olwen, still crying bitterly, and Gwilym as if his heart had stopped beating inside him.

"Dearest Olwen!" he said, "I knew it would come to this, and truly, my whole soul is sorry. God knows how I've tried to fight it, but I can do no more. Oh, Olwen, Olwen; it would have been better for you and for me if you'd let me jump into the river that morning!"

"Don't, Gwilym, it breaks my heart to hear you say that."

"Forgive me, but truly, for the sake of your father and mother, for my sake, for your own sake—forget me, unfortunate wretch that I am!"

"Gwilym," sighed the girl, "don't ask me to forget you. I never could. I have tried to, in fact, but I can't."

Each looked into the other's eyes, and Gwilym kissed the face which, to him, was almost too sacred to suffer the touch of his lips. Olwen smiled through her tears, a smile as pure as a little child's; she, who had always insisted on having her own way regardless of anyone else: something was drawing her to this unfortunate young man!

"Gwilym," whispered Olwen, "ask the men to go back to work, and stay here, don't go. My life will be worthless and pointless. For my sake, for the sake of everything that's dear to you, make the men go back, and I'll make my father give you a position—I'll insist on it—he shall have to! Oh, do this, Gwilym, and life will be lovely again—don't refuse, or my heart will break."

"Dearest, dearest girl!" said Gwilym, "I will do anything for you—I—I—I—no, I can't, I can't. I would hate myself forever: I would curse my very soul! Don't ask that of me, Olwen dearest, don't, for my sake, Oh, don't ask that of me—no, I can't. I have to take my fate as I may. Misfortune follows me everywhere I go—just forget me!"

Gwilym walked about the room two or three times, such was his distress, for even thinking had become a great effort. Olwen stood watching him in silence, but presently, she held his hand, leaned her head on his shoulder, and spoke, her voice calm, yet in utter misery.

"Gwilym," she said, "my heart is breaking. I've turned my back on everything for your sake—my mother and father, the workers, their poor wives and children, everything, I couldn't help it, I could do nothing else. But oh, Gwilym, don't go. If you go, I must come with you, and follow you, to the ends of the earth!"

"To the ends of the earth," whispered Gwilym. "Oh, Olwen, there's something sacred in your voice, just like the sound of the breeze or the murmur of the waves. It's something that comes from far, far, away, and long ago when we met before—God only knows when and where!"

Suddenly they heard a yell from the street, and Gwilym took it that some of the workers were coming.

"Olwen," he said, "the men are on their way. It's better for both of us not to let them see you here."

The girl did not answer, but she followed Gwilym to the back door in order to leave that way. Before leaving, she held out the ring for Gwilym once more, and he took it from her hand. Olwen slipped out, and Gwilym stood alone, like a man dreaming.

"Bitter fate!" he said to himself. "What crueller thing could there be? There is a world after this one. But I don't see why it isn't every man's right to live in this one; and yet why must some sacrifice themselves and lose everything, even life, and love? Something isn't right in this world. Lord God! When will You save the people—the people?"

Gwilym sat, covered his face with his hands, and wept bitterly. He cried for some time, until he heard the sound of someone opening the door. He turned to look and found himself face to face with Richard Morrus.

"Well, well," said Richard Morrus, "this won't do at all. Whatever's the matter?"

"Excuse me," said Gwilym, but I can't talk to you now."

"Come now, don't take on so; there are all sorts of trials that await a man in this world, and it does no good at all for a man to let his heart sink, and turn to crying like a child."

"If everyone in this world was able to feel as a child does, then there would be much less cause for them to weep like a child does," said Gwilym.

"I wouldn't doubt it," said Richard Morrus, unfazed, "and yet, as things are not so, one might as well take things as they are, and face them like a man."

"Yes, like a man," said Gwilym, "not whipped like a dog, or begging like one."*

"Ha! I see you've a little warm blood in you yet," said Richard, laughing loudly, a rough laugh that sent a wave of revulsion surging through Gwilym.

"The truth is," Richard added, after he had finished laughing, "that as long as men are willing to suffer, they will suffer."

"The way things are now," said Gwilym, allowing himself to be drawn into discussing a subject which never failed to interest him, "the way things are now, I don't see how they can do hardly anything else but suffer."

"That's true enough for the majority of men," said Richard, "men without a great deal of intelligence; yet there's no reason at all for men of intelligence to suffer."

---

* The original here has *nid fel gormesgwn na chynffongwn* – 'not oppression-dogs or tail-dogs' – both terms that are used in Welsh to refer contemptuously to cowards and sycophants respectively.

"Is that so!" said Gwilym. "Why, then, is it often the most intelligent who suffer the most?"

"Yes, if they're foolish enough to do so. I know of an intelligent young man, who never had so much as a sliver of advantage in terms of education or wealth, and yet who can live well enough by using his wits."

"Quite possibly—accidents happen, after all," said Gwilym.

"Accidents? Why, all intelligent men could do the same, if they only choose not to foster that sense which people call conscience, which is nothing really but stupid sentimentality. There's that young man I was telling you about, nobody knew who his father or his mother were. She died in childbirth, and he was raised by a quarryman, and put to work himself in the quarry, to start with. But there was too much steel in him to work with slate, not for him life as a slave; he went away to London, and he's getting on brilliantly, and he seems likely soon to wed a woman of no small wealth."

Gwilym had already decided from what Richard Morrus was saying that the man had somehow come to learn of his own birth and life, and had decided he would not be drawn, and yet when he heard the man all but accuse him of "using his wits" to make Olwen his wife, and describe such a thing as "getting on brilliantly", Gwilym's very soul was incensed.

In truth, he had never once thought of asking Olwen to marry him. He loved her, but his love for her was almost more like a quiet worship, with none of the ferocity which Revivalists these days value over spirit and soul. And so, when Gwilym heard these last words from the man who stood before him, he was angered to his very core.

"Here," said Gwilym, "if you were a man, or rather, a younger animal, you would answer for that with your fists.

As it is: get out of this house, as fast as you can, and remember this—say something like that about me, either to me or anyone else, and you'll answer for it, as sure as I was born. Get out!"

"Preserve us!" said Richard Morrus, "why, I wasn't saying anything at all about you. If the cap fits, well, that's not my fault."

Richard Morrus spoke these words in a tone of such sincerity and surprise that Gwilym took it that he had been mistaken, and that Richard Morrus really had been speaking of someone else. Gwilym's face must have betrayed his thoughts, and Richard Morrus saw that immediately.

"Forgive me," he told Gwilym, "if the story of the young man I was talking about is similar in some way to your own."

"I'm under no obligation to believe you nor to explain to you," said Gwilym, "and it appears to me that you're nothing but a wastrel and a coward, using your wits to live in such a way as sent many a man to prison, or even the gallows. But if you propose to use your 'wits' against me for some reason, or none, then you should take care! Now, get out!"

"I wasn't referring to you at all," said Richard Morrus, "and my purpose in coming here was to give you this."

Richard Morrus threw a package onto the table, and then left the room without another word.

Gwilym opened the package, and was surprised to find two sovereigns within. Where had they come from? Gwilym thought at first that it might have been Olwen that sent them, but then, she would never have sent them with Richard Morrus. Hadn't she urged him to have nothing to do with her uncle? And yet, perhaps she'd sent them with her uncle precisely in order to make him think that it was not her that had sent them. But no, she would never do something like that either. Who, then, could have sent them? As he asked himself this question, Gwilym happened to knock the paper in which the two sovereigns had been wrapped. There was something written on the paper. With his palm, Gwilym flattened the paper and read, in small, elegant handwriting, "For the assistance of the striking workers." Then, in similar, but slightly broader letters, "Richard Morrus."

Had he been wrong about Richard Morrus after all?

Chapter XII.
Ancient History

After he had left Gwilym, Richard Morrus walked straight to Bryn y Graig: he passed every pub on the way without turning into any of them, and went into the house, and to the room where Mr. and Mrs. Morrus were sitting, Mr. Morrus reading, his wife knitting. Arthur was out, and Olwen was in the next room singing, and accompanying herself on the piano. Richard Morrus sat on a chair by the window, and after exchanging a few pleasantries with Mr. and Mrs. Morrus, the room fell silent. Mr. Morrus resumed his reading, Mrs. Morrus resumed her knitting, and Richard Morrus resumed his thoughts, whatever they were.

Olwen sang song after song, and eventually began that sad old melody, *Dyffryn Clwyd*, and Richard Morrus suddenly turned to listen. He could hear the words clearly:

> Mor hir amdanat ti,
>   Olwen hoff, wylwn i,
> Mor unig wedi canu'n iach
>   Heb fyth gael gwrando swyn
>   Dim un o'th eiriau mwyn,
> Na syllu ar dy wedd am ennyd fechan fach.

> Ond eto wele fi,
>   Wedi'r gwae, gyda thi,
> Cawn rodio'r meysydd megis cynt;
>   A chydag ysgafn fron
>   Cawn wrando sŵn y don,
> A'r alaw bêr drwy ddail y llwyn a sua'r gwynt.

(So long, for you,
   Beloved Olwen, I wail,
So lonely after saying goodbye
   Without ever hearing the magical sound
   Of your gentle words
Nor staring at your face for even a moment.

And yet here I am,
   After my woe, with you,
We'll wander the fields, as before;
   And with a light heart
   We'll listen to the sound of the waves,
And the pure melody in the wind in the
leaves.)

Richard was listening intently, and seemed to expect to hear more, but suddenly the singing stopped, and Olwen came into the room and went to sit alongside her mother.

"Mother," she asked, "who is in this picture?"

Olwen produced a tiny photograph, and showed it to her mother.

"Oh!" said Mrs. Morrus, rather suddenly, "now, tell me, where did you find that?"

"In the middle of a bundle of old books in the library," said Olwen. "There was book of old Welsh melodies, with words written alongside some of them, and in the middle of that book I found this photograph. Who is it, mother?"

"The poor thing!" said Mrs. Morrus, in a pained voice, "it's Olwen!"

"Who was Olwen, mother?" said Olwen Morrus; "Did you name me Olwen after her? I've never heard you mention her before."

"Well, yes, it was after her we named you Olwen," said Mrs. Morrus. "The poor thing! She was like a sister to me, and indeed it was my own father and mother who raised her. Do you remember her, Richard?"

"I remember her," said Richard Morrus, "though, you'll remember I was away at University at that time."

"Indeed you were, of course," said Mrs. Morrus, "poor Olwen!"

"Did she pass away?" asked Olwen Morrus.

"I'm afraid she did," said Mrs. Morrus, drying her eyes. "Well, I say that, dear, but I'm not actually sure. The last thing we heard from London about her was that she was to be married, and then we never heard a word from her again.

"She wrote to say she was going to live abroad. I wrote to her, but never had a response. I thought at the time that she must have set off, and that she would write when she arrived, but we never heard a word from her again."

"Could I see the picture, please?" said Richard Morrus.

"Of course," said Mrs. Morrus, handing it to him. Richard looked long and closely at the picture. "Ah, yes. I remember her," he said. "She was a beautiful girl, and always happy!"

"Yes," said Mrs. Morrus, "and you know, it nearly broke my heart when she went away; but then when she wrote to say she was going to live abroad, I was quite cross, especially after waiting so long, and in vain, to hear from her."

"Yes," said Richard Morrus, deep in thought, "yes, it's all coming back to me now. And wasn't it in London that she was before she went away?

"Yes, that's right," said Mrs. Morrus, "she'd been there for two or three years."

"I thought so," said Richard Morrus.

"But who was she going to marry?" asked Olwen Morrus.

"We never did learn his name," said Mrs. Morrus. "Indeed, it wasn't until she wrote herself that we knew there was anything between her and anyone else, but we heard later that she'd gotten mixed up with a man of questionable reputation, the poor thing."

"There's no denying," said Mr. Morrus, who until then had been silent, "that was poor Olwen's curse. She was always too careless and imprudent."

"Well, I suppose that's not for us to judge," said Mrs. Morrus sadly.

"Perhaps not," said Richard Morrus, "but I remember myself hearing that she'd been associating with a man who was not of the better sort, though, as you say, Mrs. Morrus, who are we to make such judgements? Regardless, whatever it was that happened to her, from what I can remember of her, I find it hard to believe that it can have been any fault of her own."

"I agree with you, Richard," said Mrs. Morrus. "She was a lovely girl, there never was a nicer one, poor thing; I'd like to know where her grave is, if she did die, that is."

"But it's never good to be too careless," said Mr. Morrus, turning to look at his daughter, having intended the observation for her ears. As well as that, however, it was a kind of secret release for himself, for in fact he had at one time set his own sights on Olwen Williams, his future wife's adopted sister; and it was only after accepting that she would not have him that he had turned his attentions toward Hannah Edwards, whom he had found more receptive. There's no doubt that Mr. Morrus had learned to love his wife far more passionately than he had ever loved Olwen Williams, but a man does not easily forget any girl who has been so unwise as to turn him down after he has expressed his love for her.

"How awful if she was deceived!" said Mrs. Morrus. "And it's funny, her picture turning up now, so many years later! I had no idea that there was anything of hers in this house at all."

"Had she gone away before you were married, mother?" asked Olwen.

"Oh, yes, it was years before that," said Mrs. Morrus, "but it was around the time we were married that she sent me her last letter. You take care of that picture, Olwen dear. I'm very pleased that you found it."

The family all went to their beds, with the exception of Richard. He stayed up, having told Mrs. Morrus that he would be going away the following morning, and that he had no small amount of writing to do before turning in. He was still writing at some length hours later. Around midnight, he heard someone opening the front door and coming into the house. It was Arthur Morrus.

"Hullo, uncle," said Arthur, when he came into the room where Richard was writing, "you're up very late tonight."

"Indeed so," said Richard, "I am going away in the morning, and I've some writing to do yet before I go. They weren't expecting you home, I shouldn't think?"

"They weren't," said Arthur, "I hadn't planned to return tonight, but I changed my mind, and came on the last train. I suppose they've all gone to bed, have they?"

"Yes, since at least two hours ago. Shall I call the maid to make you something?" said Richard, politely.

"No, don't. I've no appetite for supper tonight, thank you. Did you do me that little favour I asked of you?"

"Yes, I did, just this evening in fact."

"Did you give them to him, into his own hand?"

"Yes, don't worry."

"And you didn't tell him that it was me that sent them?"

"No, not a word."

"Alright. Thank you, uncle."

"Don't mention it, my boy. It gives me great pleasure to do you a favour, although, I do hope you will excuse me for asking a little favour of you for myself in return."

"Of course," said Arthur, "I am in your debt, and if there is something I can do for you, then I shall do it."

"Thank you very much. I need to leave in the morning, on business. Between you and me, my funds have started to run a little low. I couldn't ask you to lend me a little? Perhaps five pounds? I'm expecting a fairly considerable sum to come my way in the next few days, and I'd be very grateful to you if you could do this favour for me, to tide me over."

"Well," said Arthur, "yes, I believe I could."

Arthur counted out five pound notes and gave them to his uncle, without so much as a shadow of an expectation that he would ever see them again. Richard thanked him politely for them, and Arthur went to bed.

Richard stayed up some time after that, busy with whatever he was writing. Once he had finished, he carefully collected the pages together, placed them together in an envelope, and put it in his pocket. He then sat silently for a moment, as if deep in contemplation. He had not imbibed as much as a drop of spirits that day, and a day without spirits was a very rare thing indeed in the tale of Richard Morrus, as could clearly be read in his face. He had managed to hold himself together fairly well that day without feeling the desire for strong drink, but now that deep, impulsive thirst had come upon him, stronger than ever. He got up and walked around the room. It was as if there were some emptiness in him which simply had to be filled; he had to drink something! He knew full well that he would not find so much as a spoonful of any sort of alcoholic drink whatsoever in the house, for Mr. Morrus and his family were dedicated teetotallers. It was now approaching one in the morning, and so the pubs would all have been closed for hours. There was, therefore, not a chance of finding anything to drink anywhere. Richard's reason told him this, but the awful emptiness burned at him, telling him that only spirits would fill it. He sat in a chair, trying to keep still, but in vain; he got up and walked about the room again. He went up to his bedroom and tried to start undressing himself for bed, but the thirst was still there, burning still. It was a great effort for him. He took off his coat and waistcoat, but then put them on again; then he drank an enormous mouthful of clean water which was in a glass bottle on the dressing table nearby. That did nothing to quench his thirst, and Richard began to prepare himself to yield to his curse and go out to look for a drink, to wake the publicans, even in the dead of night, and insist, no, *demand* that they give him something to drink! He opened the door and set off down the stairs, but his reason still told him with quiet certainty that to go out in search of drink at that time would be utter futility. He hesitated, and then turned back, shut the door, locked it, and took the key from the lock. Then he opened the window and threw the key out onto the garden path below. Then, slowly, but rather more steadily this time, he undressed, and after a little more of the water from the glass bottle, he climbed into his bed. A short while later the emptiness began to fade, and finally, he slept, poor wretch, having succeeded for the first time in many years in defeating his oldest enemy, that terrible thirst for strong drink.

He slept peacefully, and when he woke in the morning he had to call and ask for someone to bring him the key before he could leave his room. This was done, and thus Richard Morrus was freed from the cell where he had locked himself overnight. He ate a hurried breakfast, and left town on the first morning train.

Watching him go, and having realised what he had done in his effort to combat his thirst, Arthur Morrus whispered to himself,

"He deserves our pity, despite everything. What do we know of his struggle? After all, there's some good in everyone!"

Chapter XIII.
What's in a Name?

The evening after Richard Morrus left town, Arthur was making his way along the road into the countryside. The predicament of the men and their families weighed heavily on his mind. He knew well enough that his father did not see things the way he did, and he was certain that his father was not refusing the workers' request out of cruelty, nor out of any desire to oppress his fellow-men. He did not like to think that his ideas were so opposed to those of his father, and yet he felt that he could hardly be blamed for that. To think as he did was the natural conclusion of the education that his father had given him, and he could not agree with his father's point of view without completely disregarding his own conscience.

Treganol was deathly quiet. As he walked up past the quarry, everywhere he went was quiet as the grave; there was not a sound to be heard, not even the sound of the children playing happily as they usually did, and whenever a man or woman passed him on the road they eyed him suspiciously, almost as if they believed that he had something to do with their distress.

Arthur's heart yearned to reach out and speak to them, yet on he went without a word until he reached the open countryside above the town. He crossed the fields along a path, deep in thought. Presently he saw two men carrying guns, hounds in tow, coming down across the fields in his direction. They were gamekeepers, and they were on the look out, for there had been a great deal of poaching since the start of the strike. Arthur continued along the path, and crossed into another field, where, within ten yards of him, he saw three men with ferrets. It was for these men, no doubt, that the two gamekeepers were looking, and as Arthur approached them the men saw him coming, and clearly recognised him; though they did not make to leave, but rather kept on at their work, setting their ferrets into the burrows.

"You're ferreting?" asked Arthur cheerfully, hoping to start a conversation.

"It's the only way to get any meat these days," replied one of the men, testily.

"And what's it to you if we are ferreting, anyway?" said one of his companions. "This isn't your land."

"No," said Arthur, "it isn't, and of course, whether you are ferreting or not makes no difference to me. If it were up to me you wouldn't have to do anything of the sort, and, for what it's worth, nor would you be prevented from doing so. As far as I can tell you've every bit as much right to these rabbits as anyone else. But what I wanted to tell you was this: there are two keepers coming this way about a field's width away from us. Perhaps it would be better if you didn't let them see you."

The men looked at him in astonishment, then quickly started packing away their nets.

"Thank you, sir," said the man who had been testiest. "You lose nothing in trying to save a poor fellow creature!"

The three men ran off, and Arthur turned back towards the path in time to catch the two gamekeepers in the middle of a rather heated argument with another man in the next field. He approached them and saw that this other man was the young man he had met that first day he had come home, and to whom he had sent his uncle with the two sovereigns.

"I say you're trespassing, and after rabbits to poach," said one of the gamekeepers.

"And I deny it," said Gwilym, "I haven't taken a single step away from this path, and I believe that anyone who wishes to do so has the right to walk it. If you think I'm looking for rabbits, then by all means, search me, and tell me what it is I have with which I intend to catch them. I don't suppose you think I plan to catch them by running after them?"

"How do we know you haven't got some nets hidden somewhere?" said one of the gamekeepers.

"Well," answered Gwilym, "the only thing I can say in response to that is that you'd be welcome to accuse me as soon as you found nets in my possession."

"Never mind that; anyway; you're still trespassing," said the gamekeeper, angrily.

"And so I must be trespassing as well?" said Arthur, coming towards them.

"You are," said the gamekeeper, who did not recognise Arthur; otherwise he would no doubt have answered differently.

"Alright then," said Arthur, "come on, take us both to the justices: that's your duty, and the only thing you can do. My name is Arthur Morrus, Bryn y Graig, Treganol."

The two gamekeepers stared at him in surprise, and then immediately begged his forgiveness for their mistake.

"You'd better ask this gentleman's name as well, so that you can take us down together for trespassing," said Arthur, paying no attention at all to the gamekeepers' apologies.

"Well, sir," said one of the two eventually, "forgive us, but we didn't know who you were. Now, we know that you would never trespass, and as you've suggested that this man was doing nothing wrong, then we are happy to take it no further."

Arthur simply said, "Alright," and turned away, and greeted Gwilym.

"Are you coming down this way, Mr. Bevan?" he asked.

"I suppose I shall have to," said Gwilym, "as it apparently isn't safe for my sort to be walking these paths now."

"Oh, they'll leave you well enough alone now," said Arthur. "Those two weren't up to much besides making threats in the end."

"No, but they would have been different if you hadn't happened to come by."

"Quite possibly; though I would have enjoyed it if they had hauled me before the magistrates as well," said Arthur, laughing.

"And no doubt your name would have set you free there just as easily as it set you and me free here," replied Gwilym.

His tone was bitter, but not resentful, and then, as if he realised he had said something that he should not have done, he added, "Forgive me for that comment, Mr. Morrus, I didn't mean to insult you."

"That's alright," said Arthur, "I know exactly what you mean, and I agree. There's nothing on earth I hate more than the tendency in this world to trust a man, or not to trust him, because of his name or his class. And that is exactly why I would have been pleased if they had taken me in."

"The exact same reason I'd rather they didn't take me in," said Gwilym.

"Well—yes, that's it exactly. But that's just how people are. This world has grown a tail* which is much bigger than its head."

"Indeed," said Gwilym, "and a much bigger head than heart."

---

* Here again we have the usage of 'cynffon' (tail) to suggest sycophancy, an everyday usage in Welsh.

"True enough. Sometimes I think that Man has just as much growth ahead of him in terms of his mind as his body has been through already."

"And so you think he's yet to shed the tail of his mind?"

"That's it. Before he shed his body's tail, he needed to make quite a bit of use of it no doubt; and now he needs to make similar use of his mind, that it might shed its tail as well. He walks upright now, and has long since shed his tail. Perhaps his mind will one day walk upright also, and little by little, shed its own tail."

"Truly, I believe there is more truth to your words than at first glance. Perhaps there's hope for mankind after all!"

"Oh yes, there's hope. We've come a great way already, even if it took us a long time. God doesn't hurry. If He spent eons making these old rocks—the foundations of creation—then it can't be right to expect him to break his habit when it came to crowning his achievement. The time to place the capstone is a way off yet."

"Ah!" said Gwilym grimly, "you've hope and faith then, clear and bright as dawn!"

"Perhaps. But dawn isn't always cloudless either, and neither is my faith. Light and dark, brightness and shadow: thus are all things in this world."

"Indeed, and the world looks brighter to those who live in the light than to those living under a shadow! And yet, I myself have thought many times—and it's a thought that comforts me—that God is not subject to time nor means; He has no past or future tense, and no need for any means. God has space enough, space enough, and time. 'A thousand years as one day.' Yet pity poor man, upon whom time and space and means weigh so heavily!"

"And yet he cannot be without them. To man, everything is relative. He measures today according to what he experienced yesterday, and what he expects tomorrow."

"And yet the weight is sometimes too much to bear!"

"Quite often so. And yet often it is darkest before the dawn."

Talking in this way, the two made their way back to the town. Gwilym went to his lodgings, and Arthur went to visit some of the quarrymen with whom he was friendly.

Word was abroad by this point that Arthur had sympathies with the workers, and wherever he went he was looked upon accordingly with either more or less favour than before. Some of the men asked him to try and influence his father to bring an end to the dispute by coming to meet them. There were signs of suffering almost everywhere, and Arthur was greatly saddened by it all. He was one of those men who are sometimes referred to, with a measure of facetiousness, if not scorn, as being soft-hearted. Ever since he had been a child, looking upon wretchedness or suffering of any kind was certain to bring tears to his eyes. If this should be considered a flaw or a weakness, then it must be allowed that this world would be a rather more wonderful place if its circumstances allowed the propagation of such flaws and weakness; and if those men and women are believed who try to teach us that we do not cultivate men in the same way blacksmiths work iron.

His face grim and his thoughts melancholy, Arthur made his way home, asking himself why so many had to suffer, people whom, by any reasoning, had as much right to live well as he did. Was it the case that men should have to choose between starvation or working like machines, without thought or will? Gradually, Arhtur's spirits were roused to that same hot temper that would come upon him when arguing in his University's debating society, when his whole body would quiver with feeling, as if he could not withstand it.

He went into the house, and to the library. There was Mr. Morrus, sitting comfortably with a book or two before him. Arthur sat down in a chair nearby, still thinking, and presently Olwen came in.

"Father," said Arthur uneasily, "please, let me urge you to allow the men back to work—their families are suffering. It's been some time now since they were out of work, and they've every right to live as all men should be able to live. I've been visiting some of them today, and the poor little children are in a wretched way."

"Well," said Mr. Morrus irritably, turning away from his book, "as I've said before a hundred times, the men themselves are to blame. They're welcome to return to work tomorrow, if they choose to, and if the little children are suffering, well, then we must help them—"

"Father," said Arthur, "you surely don't propose to insult the men by offering them charity but refusing them work?"

"Why, in humanity's name!" said Mr. Morrus angrily, "Do tell me, what are these ideas you've got into your head? Do you think I could look at young children suffering without offering to do something to help them?"

"Truly," said Arthur, "I'm afraid that that's exactly what you're already doing, father, if you'll forgive me for saying. It's work the men want, not charity, and it can hardly be right to offer them charity but refuse them employment. I offered to help some of them today. It felt like I was insulting them, but then it isn't me that's refusing them employment. They are ready to meet you, one of their leaders told me today—"

"And who was he, I wonder?" said Mr. Morrus.

"He's a good man," said Arthur, "with none of the advantages of education, and yet he's improved himself magnificently. He's a credit to his craft, and knows the history of every country, and all about progress and man's efforts to better himself. Poor man, to have to suffer poverty and disadvantage."

"Which one of them are you talking about?" said Mr. Morrus.

"Gwilym is his name, I think."

"Oh, he's the rabble rouser who incited the men to strike——"

"Oh, father!!" said Olwen, almost without realising it.

Mr. Morrus turned his head suddenly. "Hullo!" he said, "what's the matter with you then?"

"I'm certain Gwilym didn't incite the men to strike," said Olwen, blushing.

"What do you know about him?" said Mr. Morrus fiercely.

"I know more about him than you do, father, I think, and Gwilym Bevan is a gentleman."

"Indeed he is," said Mr. Morrus, "far too much of a gentleman to be a quarryman, and he's the one who persuaded the men they should leave work."

"No, I don't think so, father," said Arthur, "I know when a man is telling the truth——"

"And so you're accusing your father of lying, are you?" cried Mr. Morrus, his temper rising.

"Not at all, nothing of the sort," answered Arthur, "but I believe that you're misjudging the boy."

"I'm doing nothing of the sort," said Mr. Morrus, "and that churl won't get any work from me, not if he begs on his knees for it!"

"Oh, father, don't talk like that, don't!" said Olwen.

"What on earth's the matter with you? What's that churl to you, I wonder?" said Mr. Morrus.

"I can't stand hearing you talking that way about the man who saved my life, and I won't stand it either!" said Olwen, bursting into tears.

"Saved your life? When?"

"The first day I went out after I was ill. If it weren't for him, I would have fallen off the cliff, hundreds of feet—"

"Oh," said Mr. Morrus, his tone extremely dubious, "funny that only now we are hearing this! I suppose that churl has been pushing his wild ideas into your head then? But just you wait. You're rather too independent. We shall have to look after you carefully from now on. It's as if there's a curse of some sort following you two! You don't for a moment count a boy like him as your equal, having been raised as you have?"

"I do," said Olwen, determined. "However I was raised, he is indescribably more than the ideas that were put in my head about working men, and he's a gentleman by his nature, rather than the kind of false gentleman that's made through wealth and ostentation, like that dandy who so often visits this house!"

"Merciful heavens!" said Mr. Morrus. "What on earth has happened to you two, to make you turn against your parents like this? Oh, Lord—"

"Hush!" said Arthur. "What's that noise?"

A bell was ringing excitedly.

"The fire bell!" said Olwen, and everyone rushed out of the room.

Chapter XIV.
A Hero's Sacrifice

The urgent sound of the fire bell had roused Treganol from its stillness. There are bells whose sound is lovely and tender, church bells, for example: their melody is a gentle, comforting sound on a summer evening's breeze. But the sound of Treganol's fire bell was one of excitement and alarm, and as soon as they heard its sound the people started to rush out of their houses, just as the Morrus family had rushed out in the middle of the argument between Mr. Morrus and his two children. The bell was located at the upper end of the town, and so it could be heard loud and clear from Bryn y Graig. The streets were full of people, running from every direction. The street in which the fire was blazing was soon discovered, and was already full of people before the fire brigade had assembled. Mr. Morrus, Arthur and Olwen arrived quickly, and Mrs. Morrus came soon afterwards, having been unable to stay put after seeing everyone running wildly towards the scene of the blaze.

Thick columns of smoke were rising above the street, such that it was difficult to tell at first exactly where the fire was. Mr. Morrus and Arthur both pressed their way forwards through the crowd, but in the general excitement neither was particularly noticed. Mr. Morrus was soon standing in front of the house where the fire was burning, Arthur alongside him. Treganol had rather ineffectual means to extinguish fires at the best of times, and in the upper part of the town, where there was little in the way of water, there was little that could be done to extinguish such a fire as was now burning before them. Presently Gwilym appeared and also made his way through to the front of the crowd to stand alongside Arthur Morrus, looking through the smoke at the burning house.

"That's poor Joseff's house," said Gwilym. "God preserve us; the children are upstairs!" said Arthur, who had just been told as much. "We must try and save them!"

"Is there a ladder?" said Gwilym. "Bring it here, now, quick as you can—hurry!"

Gwilym's voice rang as the fire bell had done above all the commotion, and soon someone was hurrying forwards with a ladder.

"Here is is!" they yelled. "Make room!" said Gwilym, grabbing hold of the ladder and setting it against the wall so that he could climb it and enter the smoke-filled house through the upstairs window, but no sooner had he done so than Arthur Morrus was climbing it, much to the approval of the crowd, who broke into applause. The smoke had cleared a little, and Mr. Morrus realised who was climbing the ladder.

"Arthur, Arthur!" he cried, "come down, you can't save them there's too much fire! Leave it—let them—oh Arthur, come down!"

If Arthur had heard his father he did not pay any attention, for before Mr. Morrus had finished shouting at him to come down he had reached the top of the ladder and was busy breaking the window with an iron bar Gwilym had handed to him. Shattering the window, he yelled, "Someone come to take the children, hurry!"

Without waiting for a response, Arthur Morrus disappeared in through the window to the smoke-filled room, and Gwilym was readying himself to follow after him.

"Oh, Arthur, Arthur, dear!" cried Mrs. Morrus, wringing her hands, but above the noise Gwilym could be heard yelling, "Wait, Mr. Arthur, let me come in!"

The crowd listened to the words, and someone was heard yelling "Gwilym!" in an imploring voice. Not even Mr. Morrus realised that the voice was his daughter's, but Gwilm heard, and recognised it. Stepping in through the window, he received one of the young children from Arthur Morrus, and, half blinded by the smoke, handed it down to another man standing on the ladder below. Arthur was still searching for the other child, at the heart of the smoke and fire, for the floorboards beneath him were quickly catching fire. Gwilym yelled at him to hurry, but the smoke was beginning to confuse Arthur, and he still could not find the child. Gwilym stepped off the ladder onto the windowsill to climb into the house again, but as he did so the fire suddenly burst through the floor, wreathing around the room and then blasting out of the window, pushing Gwilym backwards to the street with a cry, just as the upstairs floor collapsed in a fiery pile to the kitchen below, Arthur and the little child with it.

Mr. Morrus broke into unrestrained tears. "Oh, my boy, my boy!" he wailed, though in all the commotion he was hardly noticed.

Gwilym lay on his back in the street, as if dead. Olwen kneeled alongside him, and touching his shoulder, spoke his name. That seemed to rouse him, and he got up, looking about him in confusion, as if he was seeing everything for the first time. Less than a second later it all came back to him.

"Great mercy!" he said, "they'll both be burned alive!"

Gwilym turned, and calling for someone to follow, rushed in through the door to the middle of the smoke whilst Mr. Morrus yelled, "Oh, for God's sake, save Arthur!"

"Oh, yes, save, save my boy!" wailed Mrs. Morrus.

"Gwilym—come—back!"

All present heard these words, and the same moment Olwen rushed towards the door through which the thick smoke was billowing, but two or three men grabbed a hold of her and prevented her from entering.

Only a second or two had passed in fact, though it felt to all as if it had been some minutes since Gwilym had entered. They all held their breath, waiting for him to come out, and yet, hardly any of them dared to believe that anyone could come out from such an inferno alive. Within, the house was full of smoke, and as Gwilym entered he choked and fell down onto the hot ashes and debris. However, the back door was open, and as that was lower down than the floor it was drawing clear air under the smoke opposite the door, where the floor above had not collapsed, and having fallen Gwilym found that he could breathe again, and recovered a little. Crawling on hands and knees he found Arthur Morrus lying nearby on the remains of the floor. Through a great effort he succeeded in dragging him to the door, and then with a final effort and his last ounce of strength Gwilym rose to his feet, Arthur in his arms, and staggered out. He reached the door, and staggering through it he passed his burden to the hands of some men who were trying to make their way in through the smoke.

"Water, quick!" said someone. "He's dying, hurry; bring water, water!"

Someone pushed through the circle of people surrounding the two. "Here's some water," said a rough voice. "Now, just let me give it to him, God bless him!"

It was old Nansi. She kneeled at Arthur's side and gave him the water.

"He's dying!" she said.

"Oh, no, not dying, don't say he's dying, he's too young to die!" said Mrs. Morrus. "Oh, what on earth made him go into that house? If only he hadn't—"

"He saved a small child, ma'm," said Nansi. "Don't break your heart, ma'm, he's getting better, look."

Arthur had, in fact, been very badly burned, and having been revived a little by the water, he began moaning painfully. His face was terribly burned, and his clothes had been torn and blackened by the flames. He had also been badly hurt when the burning floor had fallen, and in all likelihood would have already been dead before Gwilym could reach him had the fire not by that point spread to the wood in the roof of the house, making holes which had drawn in the current of air once someone had opened the back door. Arthur groaned, and the people pressed in all around him whilst Gwilym was trying to get onto his feet, calling for someone to go in with him to search for the other child, whom most had forgotten amongst all the drama of seeing the state of poor Arthur Morrus. It was at this point that the fire brigade arrived, but even as the people cleared the way for them the roof of the house fell in with a crash.

"That poor child will be buried under it all!" said Gwilym, and the crowd looked at each other in horror at the child's terrible fate.

The doctor arrived quickly, but Arthur Morrus was dying. Nansi cradled his head, and the people looked on in sympathy and alarm.

The doctor did his best of course, but in vain. Arthur had been hurt so badly that he was beyond the help of any doctor. His groans grew ever weaker, and without hearing his father wailing nor his mother crying, Arthur Morrus died.

"Oh, it's terrible!" wailed Mr. Morrus, burying his face in his hands whilst Mrs. Morrus ran about shrieking in despair, "Oh, my foolish boy! Oh, to die here, not at home! Oh, Arthur dear!"

Though the fire brigade were busy doing their best to extinguish the blaze the crowd were mostly watching

Arthur's last moments. Gwilym bent, and, taking the young man's burnt hand, turned his head away, and began to weep like a child. Indeed, all present were either weeping or fighting the urge to do so at the heartbreaking scene.

Amongst all the commotion, a broken, agitated voice was heard at the edge of the crowd. Joseff's wife pushed her way through the crowd, yelling, half mad,

"What shall I do now! Gwen and Joseff dead, and everything burned, and my little boy in the fire! Look! That's the man who starved my husband to death—down with him!"

To a man, the crowd turned to look at Mr. Morrus, and as quick as lightning their anger rose and turned against him as soon as the poor woman yelled, "Down with him!"

"Down with him! Down with him!" The crowd picked up the chant, beginning to press all around Mr. Morrus. He seemed to hardly understand what was happening, but the men, their feelings hardened by their long suffering and roused by the fire and its terrible consequences, seemed ready to rush him.

"Down with him!" screamed Mrs. Tomos, and the crowd chanted angrily, "Down with him!", and in the blink of an eye some at the front had started moving towards Mr. Morrus.

"Now, lads!" yelled Gwilym as loudly as he could, stepping between them and Mr. Morrus. "Surely you don't want to insult the memory of this dead man who just laid down his life for the children? It doesn't become you to yell and curse above the body of one who lost his life for the sake of others. That's it, take off your hats for him—this man was a hero!"

The men stood, and removed their hats, each one, looking in silence at the dead body lying in the street before them. And so that body had saved another life, that of Mr. Morrus. The crowd's attention turned back to the house, where the men of the fire brigade had by now managed to bring the fire under control, though it had stared spreading to nearby buildings, and were now attempting to enter to search for the child's body.

Arthur Morrus's body was carried home, and the people turned their whole attention to the burned building once more. It took some time to find the child in amongst the rubble and debris, horribly burned of course. The smoke billowed still in great black columns above the site of the tragedy, and still the people gathered around, sometimes talking, but mostly just staring at the ruined building, without saying a word to one another. The people of Treganol had been visited by Death in one of its most terrible forms, and that after long weeks of suffering and hunger, and they took a moment to reflect and think. The looks on their faces showed quite clearly what they were thinking. At Bryn y Graig, the mood was of mourning. Hardly anyone in the house seemed able to understand what had happened. Mr. and Mrs. Morrus were as if dazed, and Olwen's mind also was in a strange state indeed, though neither her father nor her mother even noticed her now, let alone thought to tell her that her words and behaviour had been inappropriate or immoral.

It would be futile to try and describe how Mr. and Mrs. Morrus felt. Days went by, and the two seemed as if in a dream. An inquest was held into the deaths of Arthur Morrus and the child, and it was determined that both deaths had been a tragic accident, and the two were buried on the same way, in the same graveyard. The whole time, Mr. Morrus and his wife seemed as if they did not understand what had happened, and indeed, there was hardly a man or woman in Treganol who appeared to.

And yet, something had changed in the people's minds as a result of the fire. Joseff's widow's words had directed the quarrymen's hatred at Mr. Morrus, and the tragedy had made them feel more bitter than ever. Of course, Mr. Morrus could hardly be blamed for the fire, and in fact he had lost as much in the fire as anyone else, but the men were not in the right state to think reasonably. Mrs. Tomos's heartbreaking voice, and her angry words, "That's the man who starved my husband to death; down with him!" were a constant refrain in their ears. A storm was brewing.

Gwilym realised this very quickly, and did his best to try and calm the men, and yet although he had an influence over them still, circumstances had begun to weaken it, and some of the men had even gone so far as to accuse him of being in league with Mr. Morrus, saying that he was trying to persuade them to yield to him.

Some two days after Arthur Morrus's funeral Gwilym was in his room, turning all this over in his head. His mood was bitter, in no small part due to the suggestion that he had betrayed his comrades in some way. He had had to swallow many a bitter pill over the course of his life, he thought as he sat there on the only chair he had, but none quite as bitter as the false accusation that he had wronged his fellow man. As he was thinking this, he heard a gentle knock on the door.

"Come in," said Gwilym.

The door opened and a stranger came in, asking, "Are you Gwilym Bevan?"

"I am," said Gwilym.

"Well then," said the stranger, "I want to speak to you."

Chapter XV.
A Message from Richard Morrus

"So," said the stranger, "you're Gwilym Bevan."

"I am," answered Gwilym.

"A companion of yours has sent me here to ask you to come and see him at once."

"A companion! Why, I never knew I had such a thing as a companion in this world."

"Evidently, you do. He was quite insistent that you should come with me, immediately."

"To where?"

"To London."

"Preserve us! How do you think I could get to London? It's expensive enough to get there, even for a man who has funds to call on when he chooses."

"You are not wrong, but here; here's the money."

The stranger produced a purse, heavy with coins, and offered it to Gwilym. The stranger seemed to expect Gwilym to snatch it eagerly.

"There's something strange about this," said Gwilym cautiously, "who gave you this money?"

"He told me his name was Richard Morrus, and he was quite insistent that you were to come and see him immediately."

This was quite unexpected, and yet Gwilym immediately remembered Olwen's words, and his promise to her that he would have nothing to do with Richard Morrus. And yet, there was something strange about this request, and Gwilym had a strange feeling that he should obey this request from this stranger. He could not, however, do so without telling Olwen.

Having promised her so firmly that he would have nothing to do with the man, it was the very least he could do to tell her. Indeed, Gwilym was minded to agree with Olwen's instinct that no good would come of him nor anyone else involving themselves with the man, and he wanted to know what she would think about this strange request.

Even as Gwilym was turning these things over in his head, Olwen came in, but when she saw the stranger she excused herself and turned to leave.

"Wait a minute," said Gwilym, "I want to speak to you."

Olwen came back, and turning to the stranger, Gwilym said, "You shall have my answer if you come back in one hour. I cannot decide my answer in a minute."

The man looked suspicious, but agreed, and left him with a promise to return in one hour to hear Gwilym's answer to his request.

"Who is that man, Gwilym?" said Olwen.

"I'd like to know that myself," said Gwilym.

"What did he want from you?"

"He wanted me to go with him to London."

"Gwilym!"

"Yes, and stranger still, he offered me money to pay for the trip, from a companion who wanted to see me, he said. And who do you think that companion was?"

"I don't know. Who was it?"

"Your uncle, Richard Morrus."

"Oh, Gwilym, there's something going on underneath all this, something you don't know. Please, don't go; for my sake, don't go. Richard Morrus is my uncle, of course, but I can't bring myself to think that there's any good in him, and I'm certain that whatever his motives are in trying to steal you away to London like this, he can't possibly mean you well. Don't go, Gwilym!"

"I know what you mean, and yet, I'm not sure," said Gwilym. "The other day he came here, and gave me two pounds for the workers' fund."

"I'm sure he has some awful plan! Please don't go, dear Gwilym. If he wants to see you, and if he has enough money to send you to pay for your expenses, then why doesn't he come here himself? He must have some evil in mind, and I'm begging you, don't go. Say you won't go?"

"Well, alright, I won't go," said Gwilym slowly. "I haven't the faintest idea what he could want, but I suspect you're right, and I can't go against your will."

"Oh, I'm glad that you're not going to go! But you've a sad look, Gwilym. What's the matter?"

"Well, I needn't tell you what the matter is, Olwen."

"No, not that. Something is troubling you even more than that, I can tell from your face. What's the matter, Gwilym? I want you to tell me—tell me everything."

"Well," said Gwilym after a pause, pacing back and forth across the room, "I don't know what to do. It's getting worse. The end is at hand, I think: the shadows of fate are gathering, and growing darker, closing around me, and they're cold, like the frost at night, or a winter fog! They are weighing and pressing down on me, my dear, into my very soul, pushing down every feeling and instinct, and freezing my life out from inside!"

"Oh, Gwilym, what's the matter? What is it that makes you speak like this?" asked Olwen, grabbing at his arm, and making him sit.

"I could," said Gwilym, laying his head down on the table, "I could bear those who live easy lives, with their shallow religion and their morality of commerce. I could bear it when they misunderstood me and misrepresented me. But to think that my fellow workers, for whom I did my very best, have turned to doubt me, and think that I have betrayed them! Olwen, I feel so lonely, and it feels so bitter to think that everyone has been against me always, from cradle to grave!"

"Oh, Gwilym, don't despair," said Olwen, almost crying herself.

"So cold, so lonely!" whispered Gwilym, as if to himself, "Alone, alone!"

"Alone?" said Olwen, "what's the matter with you, Gwilym? I'm here with you, and if everyone left you, I'd stay by your side—you'll never be alone!"

"Yes, my dear girl," said Gwilym, "but everyone else is against me, and I am alone."

"But I will never leave you, not while I live—and if I should die, my spirit will come and find you to be with you, and to shine around you, like the air and the sunlight. You would feel like I were with you. You will never be alone, never!"

"Olwen!"

Gwilym's voice was deep, and his tone was longing. "I know," he said, "that I will never lose you: our souls are intertwined. And yet, in this I am alone, and nobody understands me. My comrades doubt me, after I have done my best by them according to my conscience; sympathy is waning, and I can feel it. I feel as if nobody knows my worries, even those who suffer the same circumstances as I, for they now doubt me. A man can't live without the sympathy of his fellows, any more than he can live without bread."

"Who doubts you, and why do they doubt you? Comrades? They're not comrades if they doubt you. Come away, leave them all. Comrades—enemies, more like. Come away from this place, Gwilym."

"But Olwen, where should we go, and how should we go, and to what?"

"I have sold all the rings and jewellery I had—and I had no small number of them—for fifty pounds. I have them here. Now, come away with me somewhere, I can't live here, and you must come. We'll go away, far away, where we can be happy. Fear stalks me everywhere here; I can't stay. Come away with me to somewhere where want doesn't stare at you from even the very walls of the houses!"

As Olwen was thus entreating him, Gwilym listened in silence, and then whispered, as if to himself: "If there was only somewhere to go where wealth does not mock the poverty of those who created it, where the wealthy man's greed does not gnaw at him harder than the hungry man's stomach!"

"Yes," said Olwen, "come on, get ready, I want us to go, far, far—"

"Yes, far, far!" said Gwilym, "And yet that would be a betrayal itself. The men would think I was a hypocrite, a liar and a cheat, and then your father and mother! No, I can't go; something is holding me here, as if I were bound to the place, despite myself!"

"But what good will it do you to stay here? There's nothing you can do, as you've seen."

"Yes. What is there that can be done? Everything is over. Need has fallen on the place like a judgement, and the men must go somewhere, and me with them. I could find work, perhaps, somewhere, and live happy, far from wealth and poverty, for it is on the marrow of poverty's bones that wealth preys, and grows fat!"

"Oh, you are going to come!" said Olwen eagerly, but Gwilym's despair quickly returned to his face.

"Dear Olwen!" he said, "you know nothing of the fate which you would bring down on your head by staying by my side. I told you something of my history, but not all of it. I don't know who my parents were. I could do nothing about that, but I remember how people in the place where I was raised would look at me as if I were under some curse, and now I'm beginning to believe they were right, and that a curse is placed on innocent children for the sins of the parents who begat them. God only knows how that can be just, but for the sake of everything that's dear to you, don't place yourself in the way of the curse that follows me!"

"Gwilym!" said the girl, "there's nothing that will turn me from you—I can't help it—"

"Hush!" said Gwilym, going to the door and listening.

"That's the sound of the men," he said. "They're coming this way in the street, and chanting, listen! That's the sound of hunger in their voices! I have to speak to them. Run, Olwen. I can give no thought of going away whilst they still believe I've cheated them. Don't stay here, they're sure to come here, and they will be angry. Now, go, out through the back, hurry, for my sake—they're coming—hurry!"

Olwen went, but the men did not come to Gwilym. They turned instead down a different street, and their wretched leader listened as the sound of their voices got weaker and weaker as they went further from him. Gwilym paced his room, deep in thought.

"We could go," he said to himself, "and whatever happened it couldn't possibly be worse than things as they are here, and yet—I can't! I know that the men are getting desperate; I know that some of them are starting to think I misled them, simply because I spoke on their behalf— they would doubt any man who had done the same, and I can't abandon them for that—it's only their despair that causes them to wrong me! I am afraid they are about to do something awful in the next few days. But what can I do? Certainly not leave—I have to go to—yes, I shall go to him!"

At that, there came a knock on the door, and the stranger came into the room again. The hour was up.

"Well?" asked he, "Have you made up your mind?"

"I have," said Gwilym, "and I cannot come."

"Have you considered this carefully?"

"Yes, very carefully."

"Mr. Richard Morrus is not well, and he believed you would come to him, and asked me to urge you to do so."

"What's the matter with him?"

"I cannot say, only that he is not well. All I know is that he wants to see you, and that he paid me to come here to ask to come to him."

"I'm sorry, but I can't come. Here's the money you gave me earlier. Tell Mr. Richard Morrus that I would be pleased to do him any favour that is within my power to do, but that I cannot come to London to see him. If he had told me what he wanted from me, it might have been easier for me to come. But under the circumstances, I must refuse."

The man took back the money, and, wishing Gwilym a good day, departed.

The workers were still shouting in the street, and Gwilym listened to them intently. Was there a way to avoid things getting worse? Perhaps Mr. Morrus would listen to him now. No, if he went, Mr. Morrus would immediately see that the men had been defeated, and were ready to yield, or at least that's how it would end, one way or another. He would laugh at them, and it was probably futile, and yet, Gwilym felt it was his duty to make one final attempt before things went too far. He set out, and then turned back, sitting down to think. At last, he stood, said "I'll go!" to himself in a determined whisper, and went out.

Chapter XVI.
The Minister

Whilst Gwilym was talking to Olwen in his lodgings, Mr. and Mrs. Morrus were sitting in one of the rooms in Bryn y Graig contemplating their loss, and trying to make sense of what had happened. Neither had said a word, yet both were thinking the same thing, and feeling the same grief.

Mr. Morrus picked up a book that was on the table nearby, opened it, and there he saw the name, "Arthur Morrus."

He burst into bitter tears, and returned the book to the table.

"What's the matter, Tomos?" said Mrs. Morrus.

"One of poor Arthur's books!" said Mr. Morrus, "and Arthur in his grave for days now!"

"Oh, Arthur, my dear boy, having to go to that cold graveyard at just twenty three!" said Mrs. Morrus. "And yet, 'the Lord giveth, and the Lord taketh away; blessed be the name of the Lord'."

"It's hard, hard to say that verse today!" said Mr. Morrus, bitterly.

"Yes, it is hard," said Mrs. Morrus, "and yet, 'the spirit is willing, but the flesh is weak.' Take comfort in the Lord, Tomos dear, as I myself have found strength to weather this terrible blow. The Word tells us, does it not, that 'tribulation worketh patience'."

"It does," said Mr. Morrus, "It does tell of 'patience'— for some—"

"For all who trust in the Lord, husband dear," said Mrs. Morrus, "do not despair as one without hope—"

"But my hope," said Mr. Morrus, "lies dead, dead in the cold, lonely, silent grave!"

"But God awaits, Tomos bach," said Mrs. Morrus quietly.

"He does," said Mr. Morrus, "but it is hard, hard to take comfort."

Presently a knock came at the door, and one of the maids gave notice that the Rev. Calfin Jones and Mr. John Huws, the minister and one of the elders at the chapel to which Mr. Morrus and his family belonged, had come to pay them a visit.

"Bring them in," said Mr. Morrus, and off went the maid to bring in the two aforementioned gentlemen.

"Good day to you, both," said the Rev. Calfin Jones, the first to enter the room.

"Good day," said Mr. Huws, who was in the habit of following the minister, and indeed would attend on him constantly, as a sexton might a priest.

Mr. Morrus said nothing, leaving his wife to acknowledge the two visitors' greetings on behalf of both of them.

"Good day, gentlemen," said Mrs. Morrus, "please, both of you, do sit down. Mr. Morrus and I are so very pleased to see you, and we do think very kindly of all the Friends for coming to visit us."

"Yes," said the minister, "I do hope you are both taking comfort in your hour of need."

"There is comfort, isn't there?" said Mrs. Morrus.

"Of course, thanks be that there is," said Mr. Jones, devotionally.

"Yes, thanks be for that!" said Mr. Huws.

"And yet it is hard, hard to find comfort!" said Mr. Morrus.

"Yes, yes," said Mr. Jones, "we are dreadfully sorry for your terrible loss, dearest brother and sister, and that's why we have come today to try and comfort you somewhat. As you know, the Word tells us that, 'it is better to go to the house of mourning, than to the house of feasting', and we must believe the Word, however hard it may be to understand Providence and its strange turns."

"Oh, praised be for the Word," said Mrs. Morrus, her tone half joyful, half crying.

"Yes, thanks—and yet, so hard it is to accept the way of things," said Mr. Morrus, uncomfortably.

"It is, it is, brother dear," said Mr. Huws, "and yet there will come a time when all the turns of the path are clear."

"And ourselves beyond reach, swimming in love and peace!" said Mr. Jones, with more fervour than anything else.

"Amen, amen!" said Mrs. Morrus, drying her eyes with her apron.

"Yes, amen," said Mr. Morrus, "and yet—how difficult to accept such bitter blows!"

"It is difficult," said the minister, "but we must try and accept the will of the Lord, dear brother. The brothers have passed a motion of sympathy with you and your wife, and have appointed the two of us to bring it to you today. Here is the motion passed, and you can both be assured that the brothers sympathise with you from the bottoms of their hearts—"

"Indeed we can!" said Mr. Huws.

"Yes," added Mr. Jones, "and this was the motion passed: 'That this meeting expresses its deepest sympathies with Mr. and Mrs. Morrus and their daughter in this their hour of need, and hope that they will find sanctuary in the Lord and comfort of true faith, that which they, in their adversity, possess, without a doubt. This meeting also expresses its concern that the area is suffering the consequences of industrial unrest, and that there is reason to believe at its root are Wild Ideas of a dangerous nature, such as those taught by the leaders of Irreligion in the country next to our own. Furthermore, the meeting entreats the Lord, in his great mercy, to enlighten the minds of those who have gone astray, and allowed themselves to be led by Wild Ideas, rather than meeting, in a Christian spirit appropriate to a land of the Gospel, one in whose honesty and justice the neighbourhood and the country in general have complete trust.' This was the motion passed, dear brother and sister, and I can assure you that the meeting was of a most heavy heart whilst passing it."

"I can assure you also," said Mr. Huws, "most heavy indeed, especially when it was said that some dared to doubt a man who has done so much for the cause of religion in these parts."

"Most definitely," said the minister, "but then that is the way of this, our cruel present world; so often it falsely accuses those who do good—it crucified its Saviour, and if that was how they treated Him, then what can we, his unworthy disciples, expect but mistreatment?"

"True enough," said Mr. Morrus, "but my thanks to you too, and to all the brothers for sympathising with us as a family for our great calamity. Bitter as that calamity is, your sympathy soothes the pain of grief, as the kind words of the motion passed by the brothers bring strength to man in the face of his bitter trials."

There was a minute or two of silence then, for the minister and his fellow visitor had done all that they could in terms of comfort, and yet they felt somehow as if Mr. Morrus was taking the edge off every proverb and verse they recited to try and comfort him and his wife. He was saying nothing against Providence, of course; he acknowledged its wisdom and grace in full; and yet somehow, at the end of every phrase Mr. Morrus uttered there was something which betrayed the bitterness of his spirit, and how hard he was finding it to accept his fate. The minister could feel this despite himself, though he said nothing except mumble that he hoped his friends would find strength to endure this trial without complaint.

Once he had expressed this hope, one of the maids came in, and said that there was a man at the door asking to see Mr. Morrus.

"Who is he?" said Mr. Morrus.

"I don't know, some gentleman I didn't recognise," said the maid.

One can only hope the girl was not committing a sin in answering in this way, for she knew full well who it was, but felt somehow that his attempt to see Mr. Morrus would be futile were she to tell him that. She thus referred merely to a "gentleman she didn't recognise," and left it at that.

"Show him in, then," said Mr. Morrus. The girl went back to the door and returned leading the "gentleman she didn't recognise" into the room. It was, of course, Gwilym, and when he entered the Reverend Calfin Jones screwed up his shoulders, though who can say whether he did so in surprise or contempt?

"That's the ringleader!" the minister said quietly.

"Yes, the avowed Atheist!" said Mr. Huws, also quietly.

The minister would without a doubt have counselled Mr. Morrus to turn Gwilym out immediately as a man with whom it was far too dangerous for anyone to risk conversation, but it must be allowed that Mr. Morrus was a gentleman enough in his way, and always prepared to treat everyone politely, at least until such point at which he lost his temper.

Gwilym bowed his head deferentially to the company and wished them all good day.

"Well," said Mr. Morrus, kindly enough, "what can I do for you, Gwilym?"

"Forgive me for disturbing you in this way, especially during a period of such grieving, but I wanted to have a word with you, sir, if you would be so kind."

In fact, Mr. Morrus now had far higher an opinion of Gwilym having seen his bravery and humanity on the day of the fire and its tragedy, and indeed his heart was almost ready to forgive all to the young man who had ventured into the flames in an attempt to save his son's life.

"Well," said Mr. Morrus, "what did you want to talk about, then?"

"Well," said Gwilym, "it's been some time now with the men out of work. They—look, I may as well be frank, as I've decided I must risk everything and do my best. They've been supported by those who sympathise with them, so far, but that aid is getting smaller by the day, and—"

"I should think so!" said Mr. Huws, who was very much against the men, despite the fact that he himself had grown wealthy in selling them goods, and not always of the highest quality either.

"The fact is," said Mr. Jones, "that this country is starting to tire of needless commotions like this, and furthermore, thanks to some specific factors in relation to the instigators of the strike, specific factors I need not name, the brightest and best in society are losing sympathy for the men."

"Forgive me, sir," said Gwilym, "but—well, now is neither the time nor the place to discuss the merits of the men's argument, but as a rule, men are not willing to suffer so long without a cause that they at least believe to be just. But regardless of that, it's well known enough that the men are suffering, along with their wives and their children, so much so that the men are getting desperate, and there's a risk they may do things that they would not choose to do were they not suffering the pangs of hunger and of need."

"Is this a formal deposition on behalf of the workers?" said Mr. Morrus.

"No," answered Gwilym, "I'm coming here entirely of my own accord. I can't help but feel that it's my duty to do something, and it is for that reason that I urge you, sir, please, suggest something, and I will do my best with the men."

"Yes, well," said Mr. Morrus, "you've good intentions, without a doubt, but you can hardly expect me to discuss this matter with you unless you are coming to speak on the men's behalf."

"I would like you to remember," said Gwilym, "the scale of the suffering, sir, and to prevent things from getting even worse, is there nothing you can suggest which could ease the way to an agreement—"

Mr. Morrus was softening, and yet he answered thus:

"I told you at the start that they can come back whenever they like, on the same terms as before."

"For humanity's sake, sir," said Gwilym "please, reconsider. I fear, as I have already said, that the men are getting desperate, and for God's sake—"

"Young man!" said Mr. Jones. "Don't take the Lord's name in vain, that's what makes men desperate. If the men are ready to be misled by some freethinking agitator like you, then they must accept their penance!"

"I wasn't talking to you just now, sir," said Gwilym, his blood beginning to boil, despite himself.

"And yet I am appealing to Mr. Morrus," said the minister. "As a minister of the gospel, I must do my duty, and I cannot allow anyone to take the Lord's name in vain without raising my voice in objection."

The minister looked expectantly at Mr. Morrus as he spoke these words, and was rewarded when Mr. Morrus said, "I agree, Mr. Jones."

"Of course," said Mr. Jones, "I knew that you would not wish to hear such insolence!"

Ignoring the minister, Gwilym turned to Mr. Morrus and said, "Please sir, allow me to urge you to reconsider the matter. It's true that I ask this of you in my own name only, but as you know, whatever happens now, I've been dismissed, and therefore you can see that I have nothing to gain personally from what I'm asking of you. In fact I am putting myself in danger by coming here like this, but I would rather do that than let anything worse happen. Just think, sir, of the men's suffering, or if the men in your opinion deserve to suffer, then think of their wives and their innocent children who must also suffer."

"I am truly sorry for the children, but excuse me now, let's not waste time; the terms I offered at the start are still on offer; they can return to work as soon as they like, just as before."

"What more do you want, young man?" said Mr. Jones, "you have your offer, and it is a fair and Christian one."

"In our present state of bereavement," said Mr. Morrus, "I'm afraid I cannot speak further on this matter at present."

"Before I go, I would like to remind you, if you permit me, sir," said Gwilym, "that your actions are likely to inflict a similar bereavement on many other families if nothing can be done, and done soon."

"Truly now," said Mr. Jones, "you should accept Mr. Morrus's answer. It is very difficult for him to speak to you under the circumstances."

"Indeed, I am sorry; I cannot discuss this any further at present, other than to say that the same terms are still on offer," said Mr. Morrus.

"Oh, God have Mercy!" muttered Gwilym to himself as he set off, but Mr. Huws overheard the words.

"The insolence of some of this class are rapidly driving this country to ruin!" said Mr. Huws.

Gwilym was turning to go, when the door opened and in came Olwen.

"Oh, Gwilym!" she said, running towards him.

"Olwen!" cried Mrs. Morrus, "Oh, shame on you, behaving thus in front of Mr. Jones and Mr. Huws, and your dear father and mother! Have you no shame?"

"Shame?" said Olwen, "No, I don't feel any shame. Shame for what? What have I done now that I should be ashamed of?"

Olwen burst into tears, but Gwilym whispered, "Don't despair, Olwen!" as he set off.

"Gwilym, wait!" said Olwen, setting off after him.

"Olwen!" cried Mr. Morrus, "Do you wish to bring this family into disrepute? Is this how you behave in front of our guests?"

"Dear Mr. Jones, will you say something to her; I just don't know what to think any more," said Mrs. Morrus.

"She's started believing some of that boy's Wild Ideas," said Mr. Morrus.

"Well, Miss Morrus," said Mr. Jones, "I'm sure that you respect your parents, and are willing to obey their instructions; I'm sure that you won't debase yourself by associating with all sorts of men—"

The girl's eyes blazed, and she turned them on the hapless minister. "No, Mr. Jones, I shan't," she said, "I shan't debase myself to associate with all sorts of men, and for that reason I shall leave this house until you have gone!"

Without another word, Olwen stormed out of the room, leaving Mr. Jones and Mr. Huws in shock, Mr. Morrus in indignation, and Mrs. Morrus in tears.

"Oh, Olwen, Olwen!" wailed Mrs. Morrus inconsolably.

"I don't know what's happened to the children—and the girl!" said Mr. Morrus. "Oh, why must everything fall apart? What is this judgement on everything—hush! What's that noise?"

Nobody except Mr. Morrus had heard anything.

"Calm yourself, brother dear," said Mr. Jones, "It's your loss that's effecting you."

"Quiet! There it is again," said Mr. Morrus. "Oh, what's the matter? Leave me alone, please, go. I'll be better soon. Thank you for your sympathy. I'll be better, after some quiet."

"We'd better go," said the minister. "I'm sure he'll get better shortly. It's his grief that's affecting him."

Mr. Jones and Mr. Huws and Mrs. Morrus left, leaving Mr. Morrus alone, pacing uneasily around the room.

"There's that noise again," he said to himself, "like rushing water. Perhaps it's just in my head. Oh, what's the matter with me? Now it's quiet again—shh; oh, what have I done?"

Chapter XVII.
"Down with him!"

Gwilym's fears proved well-founded, for many of the quarrymen were becoming desperate indeed, and the leaders were finding it a struggle to keep them from taking things into their own hands and giving notice to Mr. Morrus that he could no longer expect to be allowed to live in their midst undisturbed.

Worse still, at the exact same time that Gwilym was fighting their cause with Mr. Morrus, the rest of the men were meeting in the Old Quarry. Gwilym had known nothing about the meeting; indeed it was one of those meetings which take place whenever a large number of men are unanimous of opinion and feeling on a particular matter, even when it has been neither agreed nor arranged beforehand. Another time, the quarrymen would have been as sensible and reasonable as any other class of people, and would have easily seen how Gwilym could have been unaware of the meeting. But now, half-starved, losing all hope and desperate, getting them to reason at all was a challenge. And so, when they had all assembled, at first wandering in by coincidence from here and there, and later from word spreading that a meeting was taking place in the Old Quarry, some of the men noticed that Gwilym was not there.

"Where's Gwilym?" asked one to his neighbour.

"I don't know; is he not here?" came the reply.

"No, he's nowhere to be seen," said the first.

"Well," observed the other, "you'd think he'd be here, of all the men."

In this way word spread quickly, and very much in the tone of this last sentiment, that Gwilym was not present, and very soon the men showed their willingness to doubt their leader. Some of the other leaders attempted to dissuade them from such thoughts by arguing that it was certain Gwilym was not aware of the meeting, and that he would surely attend as soon as he had heard word. This quietened the men for a while, but as time wore on and Gwilym still did not appear they began to stir again and, despite the best efforts of the others, it was determined to send some half dozen of their number to search for him.

It was one of those unfortunate coincidences that the six men appointed to this task were six of the most desperate of the men, and as soon as they were named they set off immediately for their leader's lodgings to find him.

In complete ignorance that these emissaries were on their way, Gwilym was at that moment sitting in his room trying to decide what he should do next. Indeed, he asked himself, what would happen next? Despite himself, he felt once again that he had lost all faith in everything, and as if he could do nothing but wait and allow events to follow their course, one after another, as a man awaiting his own execution. Everyone, it seemed, had it in for the poor, and everyone was willing to attribute the worst of intentions to himself, a fact which was harder to bear than all the suffering and the hunger put together! Yes, everyone had turned against him, all except one. She still believed in him, and was still pure, still true, and faithful. Gwilym took out the ring she had given him, and examined it at length.

He then heard a commotion in the street outside, the sound of footsteps, and a loud knock at the door. Hurriedly, Gwilym put the ring away and yelled out, "Come in!"

A half dozen of the workers came in and stood before him.

"Where were you, instead of at the meeting?" said the first—a burly, strong man called Huw Dafis.

"What meeting?" said Gwilym.

"The meeting in the Old Quarry; they're there now, and you're sitting in here moping."

"I didn't know anything about a meeting," said Gwilym; "The committee didn't arrange any meeting."

"Committee!" said Huw, "What good are committees? They don't do a thing, and that's the truth. We're going to take things into our own hands!"

"Very well," said Gwilym, "if you think you can do better, then good luck to you, I say."

"What are we supposed to do, then?" said Huw, less aggressively this time, "Is there a way we can get food to eat? If not, then we have to do something. Some of us are going to break into the shops. We can't stand this any more, and we won't stand for it, either, that's how it is!"

"Here now, don't do anything rash," said Gwilym, "We mustn't go breaking the law—"

"Law!" said Huw dismissively, "Is it the law for a man to starve to death? Here's you, having urged us to strike, and led us into this mess, and here you are advising us to suffer and starve to death without lifting a finger, like cowards. You've sold us down the river, you have!"

"No!" said Gwilym fiercely. "I've suffered as you have, pang for pang. I've sold my books, and given every penny I got for them to share between all of us. After you yourselves chose me to speak on your behalf, and me staying here with you even though I was dismissed before the strike, and now you're telling me I've sold you out! Say what you want about me, but don't question my loyalty! I've been honest, and trusted you; I know that you and your families are hungry, as am I, but I won't have any part in stealing the property of those who've helped us through this—I would rather starve than do that—"

Suddenly, Olwen's ring fell out of Gwilym's pocket, and rolled across the floor to Huw's feet. Huw leaped on it and grabbed it eagerly, a fierce grin on his face.

"So you sold your books," he said scornfully. "Why didn't you start with things like this? You'd get enough for several meals for this! Pang for pang you've suffered, have you? Why, you hypocrite: you're lying through your teeth!"

"Huw!" said Gwilym, in a tone of such severity that the big man took a step back. "Give me back that ring!"

"Yeah, give it him back, Huw," said one of the others.

"Hold on a minute," said Huw, his confidence returning. "Didn't we agree to share everything?"

"We did," said Gwilym, "and I've sold everything, but I won't sell that ring. It's none of your business why, nor anyone else's."

"Huh, got it from some wench besotted with you, no doubt," said Huw, grinning gleefully, "I can see it now, ha!"

"Here," said Gwilym, stepping towards him, "give it back."

"Are you threatening me, liar?" cried Huw wildly, striking Gwilym's shoulder.

"Alright then, on your feet!"

Gwilym said these words calmly but threateningly, and before any of the others could intervene Gwilym and Huw were wrestling. Huw was a stronger man than Gwilym, but he was shorter, and less agile. The others tried to separate them, but Gwilym yelled, "Leave it!", and so they stood back.

That moment Olwen came into the room, screaming, followed by some more of the workers.

"Oh, Gwilym, what's this?" the girl wailed in fright. "Oh, don't kill Gwilym, please, please don't!"

"Hello, so this is how the wind blows, is it?" said one of the workers.

"Oh! Let me go, let me go, Gwilym!" wailed Huw, releasing his own grip and lying helplessly in his opponent's iron hold.

Huw yielded the ring, and Gwilym let him go, but now the others, having seen Huw defeated, were inclined to side with him.

"Now, for heaven's sake, listen to me," said Gwilym, "Let's be reasonable—"

"Let's have that ring!" said one of the workers.

"Oh, Gwilym, come away," yelled Olwen, "come away, let's go, now. Here's the money—"

"Money! Ha!" yelled Huw in wild triumph. "Didn't I tell you that's how it was! He's sold us, he's going to leave us, and here's the oppressor's daughter come with his fee! Down with him, and with her! Down with them! Down with them!"

"Oh, mercy!" yelled Gwilym, "What did I do to deserve this?"

"Down with them, down with the both of them, down with them!" chanted the men, rushing at Gwilym and Olwen.

An indescribable struggle ensued. The men yelled in their fury and disappointment, Gwilym fought tooth and nail to keep Olwen safe, Huw swore, and tore his way through his co-workers to get at the man who'd just bested him—the only one to have ever done so. Through it all could be heard Olwen's voice pleading "Oh, don't, don't!" But there was no mercy. In the chaos, Olwen fell to the floor, and the men grabbed Gwilym, pushing him out ahead of them and scrambling like wild animals into the street, trampling Olwen underfoot without thought or feeling. And off they went down the street yelling, "Down with him!" "Fraud!" "Hypocrite!" "Judas!" and many other names similar and worse, mixed with vows and curses. The man whom a little while earlier had been paraded on their shoulders as a champion was now being chased through the streets and being pelted with every insult and obscenity. They were met by some policemen who tried their best to rescue Gwilym, but they were far too few. The crowd grew, men, women, and children joining in, though they knew not why, to yell "Cheat!" "Traitor!" "Liar!"

It's doubtful any of them knew where they were chasing their former hero, and yet on they went. Presently the Reverend Calfin Jones met the crowd. At first the minister couldn't work out what the matter was, but shortly was told by someone that the men had turned against Gwilym and that he was the man whom they were cursing as a "Traitor!" and "Liar!". No doubt the minister felt that these were reasonable enough names to call a man such as Gwilym, and yet, narrow-minded as he was, the Reverend Calfin Jones was not a man to look upon his fellow man in danger for his life without trying to save him. The minister ran through a side street, and back through two other streets so as to come out ahead of the fierce crowd just as they were entering the Square at the middle of town. Mr. Jones ran to the top of the steps by the lamp-post and, removing his hat, yelled at the top of his voice:

"Stop this! Stop this! Listen to me!" There was something out of the ordinary in the preacher's voice and appearance, and many of the people did indeed stop to listen. At the same moment the policemen, along with a few other men who were willing to help them, came to meet the crowd. The minister yelled loudly for the people to stop, but the crowd was as wild as ever. Nobody knew exactly how, but somehow, in the midst of all the chaos, the policemen and their supporters managed to reach

Gwilym, and pull him to safety beyond the crowd's fury, leaving them to mass around the Reverend Calfin Jones.

"You've brought shame upon yourselves as Christians and as workers!" cried the minister, and he continued much in this vein, whilst the crowd stood to listen attentively.

Old Nansi heard the commotion, and came out of her cabin to see what was happening. She went through the street where Gwilym had his lodgings and, as she passed by the door, she saw that the window had been shattered. Cautiously, Nansi went into the house. It appeared empty, but in Gwilym's room lay the remains of a chair and table, and, by the wall behind the door, a woman lay flat, blood streaming from her face.

"Dear God!" yelled Nansi. "Who's that—Miss Morrus! What's the matter? Get up! What? Dead! Great mercy, they've killed her! Murder! Murder!"

Nansi rushed from the house and down the street, yelling still, "Murder! Murder!"

Chapter XVIII.
All is Lost

As the events of the previous chapter were taking place, Richard Morrus arrived back at Bryn y Graig. Richard, however, was now very different in appearance compared to how he had looked when leaving a few weeks beforehand. Indeed, at first he was barely recognised by the maid who opened the door. His face was pale, almost blue, his wasted body was quivering, and he could barely speak, and yet Richard Morrus was not drunk! Having understood who he was, the maid led him into the hall, where Richard sat down on a chair, groaning painfully. Shortly Mrs. Morrus appeared, and saw immediately that Richard Morrus was most unwell.

"What's the matter, Richard? Are you ill? O *bobl bach,*[*] what is it? Mary, run to fetch the doctor!"

The maid did as she had been bidden, and Mrs. Morrus tried to get Richard to tell her what the matter was, but he would do nothing but groan, and did not speak a word. Help was sought immediately, and Richard Morrus was carried into his bed, and before long the doctor arrived and gave him something for the pain. Mrs. Morrus was so occupied with Richard that she had no time to check in on her husband Mr. Morrus, who was also complaining of not being quite well.

Mr. Morrus was sitting in his study, when the maid came in with a letter for him. In truth, he had no real heart to open the letter, but forced himself to do so, and read

---

[*] *Bobl bach.* Lit. 'little people', a common expression when at a loss.

it. This is what it said, or at least, this is as much of it as
Mr. Morrus was able to read:

"Dear Sir,
I am sorry to inform you that the Mine workings at
Llan-y-Coed must be considered a failure. It is clear now
that the small vein of lead that was discovered has been
exhausted, and that there is not, according to the opinions
of those men who have inspected the work, any hope of
further discoveries. As you are aware, almost all of the
company's reserves have been spent working the vein
which has proven to be so treacherous, and thus the
company no longer has the funds to continue operation,
as no further funds were authorised in the previous
meeting..."

Mr. Morrus got up suddenly, and placed his hands on
his head.

"Oh!" he said, "I can't read any more of it.
Everything's coming together, oh, my head!"

Mr. Morrus fell down as if dead, and that very moment
Mrs. Morrus came into the room, having intended to
inform Mr. Morrus about Richard's perilous state,
although he was in fact a little better now. Mrs. Morrus
had a terrible shock to see her husband lying on the floor,
but she leaped to his side.

"Oh, Tomos, whatever's the matter?" she said.

"It's over for me, Hannah dear!" said Mr. Morrus.
"Everything's gone, swept away in an instant!"

"Oh, you must try and endure," said Mrs. Morrus.
"This is the will of Providence, Tomos bach. You'll find
strength."

"No!" groaned Mr. Morrus. "This cuts deeper than
anything I could ever bear!"

"Tomos! The Lord God is merciful."

"He is, but a misspent life is one of darkness, without hope."

"Oh, you're confused, you poor thing! You, who were so generous to every good cause, you who've done so much for—"

"Yes, yes," said Mr. Morrus, "and all in vain! The light of the fire that cost Arthur his life has shown everything as it truly is. He was right, Hannah!"

"Oh, Tomos! What's the matter with you? After all these years, and everything you've done—"

"Yes, but what was it all for? I've given my service for free, every Sunday, holiday and workday. I spoke out for equality and justice for the workers, and I believed in them, as vague ideas, as philosophies, but—but there was no money in them! I should have realised that my treatment of the men was against all the things I professed to believe throughout my life. I didn't like them treating me however they liked—I never thought about what those things I always supported meant in practice. And I know who I am now, and all is darkness!"

"Oh!" wailed Mrs. Morrus. "Think about something else, the good things you've done. Why, you've been a wonderful family man for forty years, and not even the meanest beggar was ever turned away from your door—"

"Yes!" wailed Mr. Morrus, still mercilessly venting his despair, "but the light shines through it all now! Arthur saw through me, and I called him an atheist; Olwen saw through me and I called her wanton—it was as if they lived in a different world to me. I shouldn't wonder if you, Hannah, hate me now, for I'm not the man you thought I was; it wasn't me with whom you fell in love all those years ago, but another man, completely different from the man I really am—"

"Oh, Tomos, Tomos, don't talk like that! Why, I love you just as much as ever—"

"Thank you!" said Mr. Morrus. "You're all I have left. Arthur, my great hope, is dead. Olwen has broken her heart, and now we've not a penny to our name—"

"Tomos!" cried Mrs. Morrus in shock.

"Not a penny," repeated Mr. Morrus. "The mine at Llan-y-Coed has swallowed the lot, and the strike has ruined the quarry."

"Oh! What shall we do?" said Mrs. Morrus, "Oh, Tomos, Tomos, why didn't you tell me? Oh, you've been cruel to me!"

"I know," answered Mr. Morrus. "I've been cruel to you many times, and I know that it isn't me, as I am now, whom you love!"

"Oh! What will become of us; after all these years—"

"That's it! I know that everything's over, that I've lost it all, the things I treasured most of all, but I can't blame you for any of it; though remember that I never thought it would be like this. Thought? Why, what did I ever think? Well, let it be remembered at least that I didn't intend this!"

"But why didn't you tell me it was all gone? Oh, what shall we do, what shall we do"

Mrs. Morrus scampered about the room in her grief, wailing bitterly. Mr. Morrus watched her, feeling his heart sink even deeper inside him, but Mrs. Morrus was inconsolable, and wailing, "Oh, what will become of us?" she stormed out of the room.

"There she goes," said Mr. Morrus to himself sadly. "The one whose heart and soul I'd thought were mine—gone, and me left alone, alone! Oh, where is Olwen, my child, my own flesh and blood? Is there anything left on earth which is mine? Is there one heart that loves me, one being that can sympathise with me? Oh, Olwen, Olwen!"

When Nansi had rushed from Gwilym's lodgings yelling "Murder," people had immediately begun to gather. Olwen had not, in fact, been killed, as Nansi had thought, but she was badly hurt, and unconscious. The policemen arrived shortly, and a doctor was sent for. He did his best, but Olwen was very slow to recover, and when she started to come to, and to see the people around her, she had such a shock that she fell unconscious again. The doctor commanded everyone but Nansi and one or two other women to leave the room, and the police cleared the place and stood watch by the door to keep anyone else at bay. The story that Olwen had died, kicked to death by the quarrymen, spread quickly through town; and though a fair number knew that it was not true, the truth spread far more slowly than the first story.

Word that Olwen had been killed reached Bryn y Graig. Someone told one of the maids, who rushed into the house in alarm. She did not quite know what to do, but in her confusion went into the room occupied by Mr. Morrus. He had now recovered somewhat, and had gotten to his feet, in time to see the wild-eyed, frightened look on the maid's face.

"What's the matter, Mary?" asked Mr. Morrus.

"Oh, sir, I can't say it," said the girl, "something awful has happened!"

"What, what has—tell me!" demanded Mr. Morrus, grabbing the girl's arm fiercely. In her fright, and in the pain Mr. Morrus was causing her by holding on so fiercely to her arm, the girl burst into tears.

"What is it?" insisted Mr. Morrus, still gripping her arm in his agitation.

"Oh!" said the girl. "They're saying the quarrymen have kicked Miss Olwen to death!"

Mr. Morrus very nearly collapsed. His face went the colour of chalk, and his heart stopped.

"Where is she?" he said, fighting for breath.

"In the house where Gwilym Bevan lives, they say," said the girl.

Mr. Morrus staggered across the room and went out. Sneaking along the smaller streets which ran behind the houses in which Gwilym's lodgings were, he managed to get inside, but not without having been seen by some of the quarrymen.

The news of Olwen's fate had also reached Gwilym's ears. He was in the police station, having been taken there after being rescued from his furious colleagues. The policemen were adamant that he should not leave, but when he heard that Olwen had been trampled to death he would not stay a moment longer. And so the policemen released him, after urging him not to endanger himself, and Gwilym set off immediately along the back streets towards his lodgings. As he was approaching them, however, whom did he meet but the worst possible person: Huw, the man who'd started the riot earlier that day. Huw was in a dangerous mood, and as soon as he clapped eyes on Gwilym he set off to intercept him.

"It's the hypocrite," he said, "and it looks like I've caught you again, doesn't it?"

"Don't cause trouble, Huw," said Gwilym. "It'll be better for everyone if you don't. You and your sort have already committed one murder today!"

"Murder?" said Huw. "If you think you can talk to me like that then there really will be a murder before the evening!"

As he said this Huw stood in Gwilym's way, threateningly.

"Won't you let me pass quietly?" asked Gwilym. "If you don't, then you'll regret it, and remember, I won't be merciful this time!"

This of course infuriated Huw, and he immediately went to strike Gwilym; but Gwilym had spoken truthfully when he had warned Huw that he would regret it, for Gwilym had realised now that force was his only choice if he was to get past. He lunged for his opponent, and once again a fierce struggle ensued. It was fortunate that there was nobody else in the street to see them, or perhaps Gwilym would have had to pay with his life for his decision to leave the Police Station and go to Olwen. The struggle dragged on, both men leaning first to one side and then the other, but Gwilym's grip was like iron, and his determination steel. Somehow, he had worked his left arm under his opponent's armpits, such that Huw could use neither of his arms; and with Gwilym holding his throat with his right hand in an iron-like grip, Huw could not breathe. His knees slowly bent, and he went limp and helpless in his opponent's grip. His face blackened. A few more seconds and Huw would be a corpse, but Gwilym released him to collapse, a helpless pile in the street.

"You should take care of what you do from now on," said Gwilym, turning away and heading for his lodgings.

Shortly afterwards, three or four of the others who had been with Huw when the trouble had first started came by, and found their comrade writhing and struggling for breath on the ground. When he had recovered a little, Huw accounted for his condition by saying that Gwilym had attacked him and left him for dead. This had the desired effect on the men, who became agitated, and soon determined to avenge their comrade. Huw had his suspicions of where Gwilym was headed, and as soon as he shared them with his friends they set off in their anger towards Gwilym's lodgings. On the way they met others who had seen Mr. Morrus making for the same place.

"Gwilym has sold us out, that's what's happened!" said Huw. "Just now he tried to murder me in the street!"

In their excitement the great majority of the men were ready to jump to the worst conclusions; and so they set off down the narrow street to the front door of the house in which they believed their oppressor and their betrayer were busy conspiring against them.

Chapter XIX.
The Mystery

Dr. Griffith and the women who had stayed with him in Gwilym's bare room had done their best to revive Olwen. A table was brought in, and she was laid down upon it whilst the doctor did his best, but she was still unconscious, a fact which made the doctor fear that she might be more badly hurt than he had at first surmised. In such a place, and in such conditions, it was difficult for him to do more than he had already done, and so there was nothing he could do except wait until such time as he would be required to do his duty. The crowd outside were yelling and agitating, and openly challenging the policemen who were guarding the door. The doctor knew that it would be futile to try and move Olwen with the crowd still there, or certainly whilst they were still in their present state of outrage. Dr. Griffith had tried to think of some means to move Olwen back to her own home safely, but had been unable to think of anything: they would need a very large number of policemen or others to keep the crowd at bay. There were not enough police in the whole of Treganol for such a task, and it would be difficult if not impossible to persuade anyone else to face the crowd's rage.

"If those creatures would only keep quiet, then that'd be something at least," said Nansi, who was herself beginning to tire of keeping quiet.

"Indeed," said Dr. Griffith, "I'm worried that if she comes to then she will fall back under again, she's had such a shock."

"Is there no way to move her home?" asked Nansi.

"That's exactly the trouble," answered the doctor. "If we could only get her away from here to somewhere safe and quiet, I believe she would come to before long."

"Perhaps there could be a way to get these people to leave," suggested Nansi.

"That would help," answered the doctor, "but that would be no mean feat, I'm afraid."

"Can I try it?" asked Nansi.

"You?" said Dr. Griffith in surprise. "Now, please don't think I'm underestimating your kindness, but what could you do?"

"Oh, perhaps I could do more than you'd think," said Nansi. "After all, it's not for nothing I've stayed alive in this old world for over sixty years."

"Well," said the doctor, "let's hear your idea, then."

"What I'd do," said Nansi, "is I'd go out the back here, and to the end of the street, and then I'd start yelling murder or something to draw their attention, and then run away. They'd be certain to come after me, sure as I live and breathe."

"But if they caught you, then I'm worried that you wouldn't live and breathe for much longer," said the doctor.

"Quite possibly," said Nansi, "but I wouldn't mind that much—after all, my life isn't so wonderful that I'd feel a great need to preserve it."

"Well, well," said the doctor, looking at the poor old woman with sympathy. "You're most brave and most kind, Nansi, but I wouldn't want you to pull these people down upon yourself."

"Well in that case you're the only one in the world to think that highly of an old woman like me," said Nansi, "but I'll give it a try, if you like."

"No, best not," said Dr. Griffith. "Perhaps they'll tire soon, and go away of their own accord. They'll have had enough soon, for sure."

"I hope they do," said Nansi, "but I'll bet you've never seen people clear out as fast as they would if someone gave one yell of 'murder' down the other end of the street. Best I go, doctor."

"No, better for you to stay," said Dr. Griffith, "I might need your help here, and besides, they've sent for more policemen, so I hear. They'll be here any time, and then it'll be easier for us to do something."

"Policemen!" said Nansi scornfully. "Why, you may as well use one old woman rather than another!"

Dr. Griffith smiled, but eventually persuaded Nansi that it would be better not to try and fool the crowd, and Nansi agreed to stay until salvation came from some other direction.

At that moment, someone crept up to the back door, and knocked on it gingerly. One of the other women went to look through the window and came back with the news that Mr. Morrus was there.

"Are you sure it's him?" asked the doctor.

"Yes, certain," said the woman.

"Well, let him in then, as quietly as you can."

The woman opened the door, and, slow and frightened, in came Mr. Morrus. He had a dazed, confused look, as if he was finding it hard to understand exactly where he was, and who was with him. He stared carefully at the doctor, and then at Nansi and the other women, and then around himself at the room, as if he were searching for someone else. He had not noticed the table, where his daughter was lying, as the doctor and the women were standing between it and him.

"Where is she?" said Mr. Morrus in a frightened squeak.

"Don't excite yourself, sir," said Dr. Griffith, "I'm afraid to have to say that there's been a very serious accident—"

"Oh, let me see," said Mr. Morrus.

"Oh! Olwen dear, they've kicked her to death!"

"Try and calm down, sir," said the doctor, "I don't think they've kicked her at all. From the looks of it she fell and was trampled underfoot. I'm hoping she'll recover shortly. She's had such a shock though that it could take her some time to recover. Try not to make any more noise than you need to—there's more than enough coming from outside. We should try and get her somewhere quiet, but I'm afraid it won't do any good to try and move her at the moment."

"Oh," said Mr. Morrus, "I've lost everything!"

"Not at all, she'll recover soon enough," said the doctor.

"Thank God!" said Gwilym, who had come into the room whilst the doctor was speaking. "Oh, doctor, is she badly hurt?"

"She is," said the doctor, "I'm afraid to say that she's been very badly hurt, but if undisturbed, and if given sufficient care and quiet, I've every hope she'll soon be out of danger."

"Oh!" cried Gwilym, bending over the table to look at the girl's pale face. "Oh, the curse that follows me everywhere has found her, she who was so pure, so innocent! If only I'd never—"

Gwilym stopped himself, and looked again at the pale face, whilst Mr. Morrus stared at him, like a man in a dream. What on earth did this young man have to do with his daughter? And yet, Mr. Morrus could not now look at Gwilym except as a being of a higher order than himself. There was something so certain and secure in him, as if he were ready for anything, always quiet and unafraid, in the midst of all the disquiet and trouble; whilst he himself spent almost every moment in fear of that great mystery which seemed to be filling him up, and to be about to cover his head and drown him forever! Mr. Morrus now looked at the poor young quarryman with admiration. Was Gwilym not a man, like Arthur Morrus, who could face death without fear?

As these things and a thousand more rushed through Mr. Morrus's brain in one great torrent, they heard a shouting in the street, loud and angry, and then the sounds of a struggle. A great fear overcame Mr. Morrus.

"Oh, if only I could die and escape!" he said, covering his face with his hands.

The commotion outside grew louder, and loud voices were heard, as if men were rowing and arguing with one another.

"He's in there," said a voice. "I saw him go in myself!"

Then there came a beating at the door. Huw and his hot-headed comrades had arrived, and were trying to make their way in, despite the policemen and those of their colleagues who were more moderate.

"He's in there, and we need to get him out," said a voice which Gwilym recognised as Huw's, understanding immediately that it was himself to whom the voice was referring. Mr. Morrus on the other hand assumed the voice had been referring to him, and once again he was overcome with terror.

"Quiet!" wailed Mr. Morrus, "they're coming, they're breaking down the door. Oh, save me, save me from them. They'll kill me, save me!"

"Flee, then!" said Gwilym, in a mixture of scorn and sympathy for the poor wretch that was appealing to him for salvation.

"Where shall I go?" said Mr. Morrus. "No, they'll kill me too. Shh, here they come; they're breaking down the door. Oh, have mercy, have mercy, save me!"

"So you're scared of dying? Flee, then, run for your life!" said Gwilym.

The men outside were beating at the door, and still Mr. Morrus begged for someone to rescue him. He was quivering like an aspen, and the doctor was watching him in alarm. The door was quivering also, as if it were about to break. Gwilym went to set his shoulder against it, and, pointing at the back door, yelled at Mr. Morrus,

"Now! Go! Flee, as fast as you can!"

"Where should I go? Oh, save me! Someone must come with me, or they're sure to kill me!" said Mr. Morrus, wringing his hands in fear and pacing about the room as if he were willing the floor to open up and swallow him, safe from the rage of the men outside.

Still the men beat at the door, yelling for those inside to open it.

"Hurry," said Gwilym. "If you want to escape, go. They're sure to push this door open; I can't hold it back. Go, now, out through the back!"

At last Mr. Morrus set out through the back door, just as the men outside began to push the front door open despite Gwilym's efforts. But someone had made their way round to the back, and when Mr. Morrus went out he came almost face to face with them. With a wail of terror, he turned back and rushed into the room just as Huw and his comrades broke down the door and knocked Gwilym over into the middle of the room, as if dead.

Huw and his fellows rushed in immediately upon opening the door and were ready to leap on Gwilym at once before he could get up, but the doctor stepped between them.

"Here now," yelled Dr. Griffith. "If you've an inch of humanity, you'll get out of this room, right now. This young woman's life is in danger, and here you are rushing in like a pack of animals!"

"We need to get at that cheat," said Huw, pointing at Gwilym. "He's sold us and betrayed us, and he tried to murder me in the street today."

The policemen were now working their way into the room between the people filling the doorway, but Huw and his fellows were closer, and still approaching Gwilym threateningly.

"Now then, you lot, get out like I asked, or I'll have to ask the policemen to clear the room," said the doctor, perhaps without considering that threats like that might make things worse.

"Clear the room!" said Huw. "We'll clear the room as soon as we get a hold of the traitor!"

As he said this Huw leaped forwards towards Gwilym, but suddenly someone stepped in front of him, and pointing a pistol at Huw's head, he said, in a hoarse stammer,

"Stand back! The next one to take a step forward is a dead man!"

The speaker was shaking, and his voice was shaking, but the pistol was pointed at Huw's face, and so Huw and his supporters fell back towards the door. This all happened so suddenly that at first nobody knew who the man with the pistol was. Gwilym looked at his saviour, and despite the great transformation he had undergone, he recognised him.

It was Richard Morrus!

Chapter XX.
The Light

Although Richard was now only a ghost of his former self, and though his face was pale and his eyes had sunk deep into his skull and his limbs had shrivelled to mere shadows, his sudden appearance, his otherworldly voice and the implement in his quivering hand put a great fear in the hearts of Huw and his impetuous comrades. They quickly retreated to the door, where they were met by the policemen who had been called into the town to restore order. Before long they had dispersed the crowd from the house, and shortly afterwards, under their care, Olwen Morrus was moved to Bryn y Graig.

Having arrived the doctor did his best for her, but the shock and her injuries were more than she could stand in her weakened state. Despite the doctor's best efforts it took her a very long time to awaken from her unconsciousness, and when she finally came to it was clear that her recovery was merely the last flicker of her candle's flame before being extinguished for good.

Gwilym went with them to Bryn y Graig. Not even Mr. Morrus objected to that. Indeed, he was now afraid of Gwilym; he was, in his eyes, something more than human. Was it not now two or three times that Mr. Morrus had seen him face death without fear and perfectly calm, as quietly as if he were bathing in the sun's gentle light? How else to explain his firmness and solidity? Who was this common quarryman who was so much more than everyone else around him? What was this power in him which enabled him to face the fires of hell, to meet the wrath and vengeance of the people, and to stand before his own threats without flinching nor showing the slightest sign of fear? Fear? Fear could not touch that man's nature; he faced every danger without it, just as Arthur Morrus had faced his own death trying to save the lives of little children, and yet he had a remarkable tenderness about him at the same time: this was no impetuous masculinity. Mr. Morrus feared Gwilym, and yet at the same time he felt that he himself could not be safe from the people's wrath anywhere but by his side! This was the young man who had told him to his face that he was guilty for Joseff's death; and hadn't he been telling the truth? If he had listened to this young man in the first place, would Joseff have died, would Arthur have lost his life in the fire, would Olwen have been mortally wounded, or so it appeared, by the people in their fury; would he himself have lost everything, as if by a single blow of vengeful fate? This is the man called an atheist by those who professed themselves to be a medium between God and man, and yet he was so unlike a man without faith; so calmly he faced every danger, the very dangers which any moment could send him through the dark curtain to meet the One who governed and judged the whole world! Despite his shock and his fear, Mr. Morrus could not stop thinking such thoughts.

And yet his troubles were only just beginning, for Olwen, though she had awakened, was quickly slipping away despite the best efforts of the doctor and his medicines. Olwen Morrus lay in the darkened room on an expensive bed, with its brass frame and fine curtains of good material and fine workmanship, and yet death was coming, slowly but surely. Dr. Griffith stood at one side of the bed, Mr. and Mrs Morrus at the other. Olwen had seen them, and had said a few words to then, and then fallen silent again. Her face was very pale, like marble, but at the centre of each cheek were two tiny patches of red, like burning fires. Her eyes were bright and still. Now and then they would turn, but slowly, so terribly slowly!

Mrs. Morrus was crying quietly, and Mr. Morrus stared at his daughter without realising where he was, nor what was happening there before his eyes. Dr. Griffith wore a pained expression, as of one man watching another drown before his eyes without being able to move a muscle to do anything to save him.

There was a long silence. The only noise was Olwen's heavy breathing and the sound of Mrs. Morrus fighting the urge to wail with despair. Presently some people walked past the house, yelling loudly. Olwen turned her head to listen; shuddered, and then asked,

"Where is he?"

"Where is who, my love?" said Mrs. Morrus.

Olwen's lips moved, but she could hardly be heard, until Dr. Griffith bent down to hear her whisper, "Gwilym."

"She's asking for the young man who was with us earlier," said Dr. Griffith. "What was his name, Gwilym, wasn't it?"

"Oh, bobol bach, she's confused, surely," said Mrs. Morrus, "please try and calm her, dear doctor."

Without saying a word, Mr. Morrus strode across the room and went out quietly. He went down into the kitchen and a short while later returned, bringing Gwilym with him.

"Here he is," said Mr. Morrus "and now no one can say I refused my child's last request!"

Mr. Morrus turned his face to the wall, and burst into tears. Mrs. Morrus stood watching, even more surprised than she was worried; the doctor's face turned gentle, as if with sympathy and pity; Gwilym kneeled by the bedside, and took hold of Olwen's hand.

"Gwilym," said she, "I'm going."

"Oh, no, you'll get better very soon, my love."

"No. I'm not going to get better, not ever. I'm going, and I must leave you."

"Not for long, perhaps."

"Oh, Gwilym—Gwilym—"

"Is everything alright?"

"Yes. Somehow, I don't mind going. Dying is easier than I had thought it would be!"

The tears flowed from Gwilym's eyes, but he took the girl's hands in his own, and said in a low whisper, 'And death is the dawning of endless light!'"

A smile crossed Olwen's face, she closed her eyes, and there was silence.

"We had better go," said the doctor, "there's nothing more we can do for her."

"Oh! What is it? Doctor, doctor, what do you mean?" said Mrs Morrus.

"She's gone," said the doctor.

Mr. and Mrs. Morrus's cries filled the house.

"Gone!" said Gwilym, standing up, and gently kissing the pale face. "Olwen—gone," he said, walking slowly from the room. Yes, Olwen had gone! Night had fallen, and the town was silent. Gwilym went out, but before he had walked a dozen steps along the road, one of the maids at Bryn y Graig came hurrying wildly after him.

"Oh, come back!" she said. "Come back, you're needed!"

"What's the matter? Who needs me?" asked Gwilym.

"Mr. Morrus—Mr. Morrus."

Gwilym remembered that Richard Morrus had saved him a few hours earlier from the people in their fury. Why had he done that? And what did he want now? He turned back into Bryn y Graig, trying to imagine what could possibly be the matter. He followed the maid back into the house, and she led him to a room where Richard Morrus was lying on a bed, the doctor now by his side. Richard Morrus looked calm and alert, but he was paler even than before, like a ghost. As Gwilym came in, he turned to the doctor.

"Here he is; you can go now, doctor," he said.

Dr. Griffith nodded his head, and went out.

"Lock the door," said Richard Morrus.

"What for?" asked Gwilym.

"I have something to tell you that won't do anyone else any good to hear, and I don't want anyone to disturb me in the telling of it. Lock the door."

Gwilym locked the door, and then sat down in a chair at the bedside.

"Many years ago," said Richard Morrus, "I was at university, training to become a doctor. In those days my father and mother were alive, and my brother Tomos was at home with my father, helping him look after what business he had. Tomos was good friends with a family who lived in this area, quite well-off, and they had two daughters—at least, one was their daughter, and another they had adopted. Olwen was that one's name, and they loved her just as if she had been their own daughter. She was a good girl, beyond compare, nothing like her beauty in the neighbourhood, and as for what was inside, there was nothing like it in any other girl on earth. As I said, my brother Tomos was friends with the family, and so I came to know them too on those occasions when I came home from my studies. This was many long years ago, but I remember what happened well. Olwen disappeared, and they never heard from her again, but I know some of what happened, even though nobody else does. She was your mother—"

Gwilym leaped up in alarm, but steadied himself, and sat down again.

"And who was my father?" he asked.

"I was." The two men looked at one another for some time, without saying a word. Presently, Richard Morrus put his hand on his son's shoulder, and began speaking again, stammering in a more agitated tone than before.

"Gwilym," he said, "I may as well call you by that name—I was never man enough to give you any other— will you forgive me for my sins? Perhaps it'll be easier for you to do that when I tell you the rest of the story. At that time, when I came to know Olwen Williams, I was a respectable young man, with very good prospects indeed. I was very fond of her, but nobody knew of our love for one another, as her parents were against her having anything to do with anyone. We used to write to each other, and we would meet in secret whenever I came home, and sometimes more often than that. But I wandered astray; I started gambling, and that led to drinking, though Olwen knew nothing about it. I would sometimes regret it all and decide that I was going to tell her everything, and reform myself, but I never could. At last, she came to London, where I was at the time, and we were quietly married, but I didn't want to make it public at the time as I was in financial difficulty. I decided it was best to leave the country, and that we let our families know that we'd been married. But as it turned out—God forgive me for what I did—things happened that got in the way of all that. I had taken to drinking heavily, and I had wagered and lost hundreds of pounds. I found means to pay my way and meet my obligations—better that I don't tell you how exactly. It's enough to know that the law does not permit such means, and so I had to escape its reach when the first chance came. And so I did: I went away, and had barely enough time to tell Olwen to send some story home so that she could come after me, without letting anyone know that she was my wife. A little while ago I found out that she had written home to say that she was about to be married to someone, and that she was going abroad with him, but the poor thing! The truth was even worse than that. I was wandering the world from place to place; drink had made me such a wretch that I never sent her a word, let alone any money that she might be able to follow me. I was like that for years, living as I could from gambling and playing cards, and drinking so much I'd become a slave to the drink. At last, having wandered from one place to another, and having been to every gambling and opium den in San Francisco, Chicago and New York, and all those places in Southern Africa where scoundrels go in search of gold, I came home again. I had had a run of good luck, and I had some five hundred pounds to my name when I set off back towards *yr Hen Wlad.*[*] Do you remember when I came here? I'd been spending time before then trying to find out what happened to my wife, and I'd found that her heart had broken having gone so long without hearing from me. She had come to Wales, to go home I imagine, but the poor thing, when she was in — you were born, and she died. Her grave is there, without a stone upon it before last week—I had one made for her, and last week it was set in place. That's where you were raised, and nobody there knew who your mother was. And oh, Olwen was faithful to me until the very end, whilst I was staggering drunk through the streets of America having forgotten everything about her! But once I'd found where she was buried all I could find out about you is that you'd gone to London some years earlier. I couldn't find a word of you there, and you must forgive that I hadn't the same interest in you as I had in

---

[*] *Yr Hen Wlad.* The Old Country: Wales, of course.

your mother—I'd never even seen you. So I came here to stay with my brother, and that very day I saw you in the graveyard, and recognised you at once. I managed to find out something of your background, and I knew for sure then that you were my son. And then the strangest transformation came upon me, especially when I saw a picture of poor Olwen in this very house one evening. I decided I would put things right for the wrong I did to your mother and to you. It took me a great effort, but never mind that: here they are, safe for you. I ask only your forgiveness; not your gratitude—I don't deserve gratitude. But here is your inheritance from your father; take it, don't say a word about it to me again; do whatever you want with it."

The old man handed a fistful of banknotes to Gwilym. "Here," he said, "five thousand pounds—"

"Where—"

"Don't ask; do what you like with it. Do you forgive me—can you forgive the father who forgot you?"

"I can, father, I can forgive you with all my heart, but I cannot accept this without knowing where you got it from."

"Ah!" said the old man bitterly. "But then I suppose that's the end of the path I've walked—nobody trusts me! Rest assured that this money was earned honestly, by myself, for you. Keep it until tomorrow, and then I shall tell you all about it; I'm too tired to tell tonight. Come to me tomorrow morning; I'm tired now, I must sleep. Good night,"

His voice was weak, his appearance tired, and he spoke as if every word was an effort.

"Good night. I'll come again to look for you in the morning," said Gwilym, and left the room.

Richard Morrus was his father! Gwilym went to his lodgings but did not sleep that night. The following morning Richard Morrus was found dead, splayed across the bed with an empty bottle of whisky on the bedside table. His desire had overcome him at last, despite one last effort against it.

Chapter XXI.
The Great Deed of Gwilym Bevan

News of the deaths of Olwen and Richard Morrus spread quickly, but hardly anyone in the town seemed able to explain what had happened over the previous few days. Those days and their wild turmoil had swept across the place like a great wave, leaving everyone in a kind of dazed excitement. There was an inquest on Olwen Morrus's body, and the twelve men called up spent almost a whole day questioning and cross-examining the witnesses, but such was the confusion, and so quickly had everything happened that no verdict could be brought against anyone that could stand up. Nobody had been seen striking Olwen nor mistreating her at all; nobody had been heard threatening her beyond yelling "Down with them!" at her and Gwilym, and the doctor testified that she had been trampled underfoot during the uproar when the men attacked Gwilym.

Gwilym himself was the most important witness, and he was questioned at length. It was put to him that the men who had attacked him had caused Olwen's death, but Gwilym testified that he had not seen anyone attack Olwen herself, and said that it was his belief, as it was the doctor's, that it was by accident that she had come to harm. And so, after much questioning and consideration, it was determined that Olwen Morrus had died as a result of the injuries and the shock sustained, but that it could not be proven that anyone had deliberately harmed her.

That evening Gwilym went home and went to bed, sick in body and in heart. The long hardship he had suffered and the sheer weight of his losses had broken the man's spirit.

Olwen and Richard Morrus were laid to rest on the same day, in the same graveyard, a short distance from one another. There were only a few companions at the funeral, but the whole town was silent, unnaturally silent. The funeral procession through the streets quietened even the most furious spirits. Gwilym got up from his bed to attend the funeral, but had to be carried back, for the effort was too much for him.

Silence once again fell on the town, as has been said. The men, who had been so fierce, were now so bitter as to be become sullen, for though a rumour spread that work in the quarry would soon restart, their wounded feelings on the subject were mixed. Gwilym had not been seen since the day Olwen and Richard Morrus had been buried; since then he had been ill in bed, and the other workers barely dared mention his name, even to one another. Some days went by, and the rumours that the quarry was to open again grew. Nobody knew where the rumours had begun, and yet there was barely talk in the town of anything else.

Late one evening, when the town's starving residents were mostly asleep, Mr. Morrus could be seen making his way carefully towards Gwilym Bevan's lodgings. Mr. Morrus did not know why Gwilym had sent for him, but could not now have refused any request from that young man. He arrived at the house and went up to Gwilym's side. The two spoke at length, and when he left, Mr. Morrus knew who Gwilym Bevan was.

The following day, Mr. Morrus struck an agreement with his workers, and work began again at Craig y Coed Quarry. The town became lively and cheerful once more, and soon enough the laughter of healthy children was heard on the streets, as it had been before the strike.

And what of Gwilym and his five thousand pounds? The first Sunday after work at the quarry had started up again, Huw, having money in his pocket at last, and having endured a long period of forced abstention, had celebrated by drinking the beer he could now buy with the previous day's wages. He was not drunk, and yet not quite sober either, and was in a rather bad temper as he walked along the street outside Gwilym's lodgings. He stopped to look at the house, remembering his quarrel with Gwilym. Just then, a tiny child came to the door, which was open a little, and cried out, "Mam!"

"What's the matter, young lad?" asked Huw.

"Uncle Gwilym's crying," said the child.

"Where's your mother?" asked Huw.

"Gone out," said the child.

Huw went into the house, and followed the child to Gwilym's room. He came out shortly afterwards, his face as white as chalk.

"Good God!" he said, "Gwilym's gone!"

Huw broke down into tears.

Soon enough the whole town had heard the sad news and, just as it had been with Huw, the other quarrymen had cried when they heard, though they did not know that it had been the dead man's Great Deed which had brought them work and sustenance once again, and that it was the compensation from the prodigal father to his son that had provided the capital Mr. Morrus needed to restart work at Craig y Coed!

Gwilym was buried in the churchyard in Treganol, less than two yards from where Olwen lay, and not far from Gwen bach's grave. According to his wishes, which he had expressed to Mr. Morrus, only the Lord's Prayer and a few verses from the Sermon on the Mount were spoken above his grave, and those by the Reverend Calfin Jones, who did so gladly. The Quarry choir sang the piece which had been sung that Sunday evening when Gwilym had made his memorable appeal on behalf of the colliers, and with the glorious sound of that final magnificent sentiment, "And death is the dawning of endless light," the pallbearers scattered.

When everyone else had cleared from the churchyard, a stranger came and stood above the freshly dug grave, removing his hat.

"And here it ends," he said to himself sadly, "but he's gone—to the light!"

The gentleman stayed there for some time, but at last he turned and went on to stand by the grave of Richard Morrus.

"And here lies my old fellow-student," he said to himself. "Ah! Life is full of mystery!"

The stranger turned and left the lonely churchyard, and as he walked along the road towards the station, a few recognised him as the man Gwilym had been seen talking with that Sunday the colliers had sung on the Square. As he had promised, the Professor had come looking for Gwilym, and to offer him a job to which he would be suited, but he was too late! He was too late also tell the son of his prodigal father's final sacrifice. He was the only other one who could have told the story. Some time earlier, the Professor had been crossing over from the Continent. One of the other passengers on the ship had fallen ill and, being a doctor, the Professor had gone to attend to him. It was Richard Morrus, and the two recognised one another at last. They had been students together, back when Richard's prospects had been as bright as his companion's. Their old friendship rekindled. Richard told him most of his story, and once he had discovered that the Professor knew his son, he had told him the rest.

"I did him and his mother wrong," said Richard Morrus, "God forgive me! I want to make it right."

"To make it right?"

"Yes, exactly. I have money to leave him—"

"Oh, yes. Well, if he knew that you'd made it by gambling, I doubt he would ever accept a penny of it."

Ricard's face turned pale. "Alright then," he said. "Then he shall never know!"

And, as you know, he never did.

There is no need to say any more, for Gwilym's story has been told. Gwilym has gone, his Great Deed is done, and the lesson of his life is there to be read by anyone who loves his fellow man.

"And now abideth faith, hope, love, these three; but the greatest of these is love."[*]

"Greater love hath no man than this, that a man lay down his life for his friends."

THE END

---

[*] Here is the only place I have deviated from King James, for in William Morgan's Bible the word here is *cariad,* love, as it is in many other English versions; KJ has 'charity' of course, but love in the second quotation, losing the connection Gwynn clearly wanted to make.

Now Available from www.melinbapur.cymru

Llyfrgell Gymraeg (Welsh Classics in Welsh)

Mary Oliver Jones	Nest Merfyn
T. Gwynn Jones	Lona
T. Gwynn Jones	Gorchest Gwilym Bevan
T. Gwynn Jones	Enaid Lewys Meredydd
W. D. Owen	Madam Wen
R. Silyn Roberts	Llio Plas y Nos

Clasuron Byd (World Classics in Welsh)

Emile Souvestre	Bugail Geifr Lorraine
H. G. Wells	Y Peiriant Amser

Translated from Cymraeg
(English Translations from the Welsh)

T. Gwynn Jones	The Great Deed of Gwilym Bevan

Keep an eye out for more exciting books coming
soon from www.melinbapur.cymru

www.melinbapur.cymru

Follow us on / Dilynwch ni ar:

X (@melinbapur)
Facebook (@melinbapur)

www.ingramcontent.com/pod-product-compliance
Lightning Source LLC
Chambersburg PA
CBHW040530170726
48295CB00012B/405